I'm a Therapist, and My Patient is In Love with a Pedophile

---

6 Patient Files From Prison

Dr. Harper

This is a work of fiction.

Names, characters, businesses, places, events, locales, and incidents are either the products of the author's imagination or used in a fictitious manner.

Any resemblance to actual persons, living or dead, or actual events is purely coincidental.

DEDICATION

For my two wonderful beta readers, who rated this book
one A+ and one vomit emoji.

THE PRISON FILES

In this folder, I have shared six of my
patient files from prison.

Every file is connected by a company retreat from my
past. I have scattered my notes about this unsettling day
throughout the book. Hopefully you'll connect the dots
faster than I did.

I must warn you, prison was more brutal than I expected.
Yes, the inmates were manipulative and dangerous — but
I also encountered a monster in myself.

By the end of these files, you will know my greatest secret
and my greatest shame.

You will learn the worst thing I have ever done.

PATIENT FILES

Pedophile Love   17

HIV Infections   47

Unusual Addiction   69

Cannibal Conscience   85

False Flag   113

Human Trafficking   137

You're Invited to the Dr. Harper Therapy Company Retreat

Ready for some beach therapy? Join us for a fun day of waves, sand castles, and veggie burgers. Be sure to pack a bathing suit! Please RSVP by end of business week.

I put down the flyer and glanced at my assistant, Noah. "What is this?"

"Our first company retreat!" he said eagerly. "Lots of places do it. It's a way for employees to bond outside of the office."

"No, I'm familiar with the concept," I said. "But — we're the only two employees."

"Well, yeah!" he said, cheeks going pink. "But bonding is important for small businesses too. Here, I got us some corporate gifts for the big day."

He tried to empty his bag on my desk but accidentally dumped most of it on the floor.

"Noah, this is—"

"SPF 80!" he said, scrambling to pick up bottles of sunscreen and drugstore sunglasses. "They say it doesn't make any difference after SPF 30, but my skin is pretty sensitive, and I feel like it can't hurt to go higher, you know?"

"Noah—"

He looked up from the ground with an anxious smile, beach items falling from his arms.

"Yeah, doc?"

I sighed, trying to ignore his excitement about the idea. But once again, I found the words coming out of my mouth in stark disagreement with my better judgment.

"It sounds... fun. Thanks for organizing it."

His eyes lit up. "Really?"

"Sure," I said. "But it's almost 9am. I need to get ready for our patients."

"Oh, right, of course!" he said, rushing to the doorway. Then he turned around. "Wait, just one more thing."

I looked up from my notebook. "Yes...?"

"Can you RSVP—" He hurried back over and put the flyer back on my desk. "For planning purposes."

I glared at him. "Are you serious?"

He held out a pen to me.

I rolled my eyes, grabbed the pen, and circled:

SHORE!

We found a small break in the sea of people and set down our chairs.

I reached into my bag and pulled out a book, but I wasn't even able to get past the first page before Noah stood up and bellowed:

"WELCOME TO OUR FIRST ANNUAL—"

He spun around dramatically and accidentally kicked sand in my face.

"Oh, sorry!" He handed me his towel and lowered his voice. "Welcome to our first annual company retreat—"

"Wait, there are going to be more of these?" I said, wiping the sand from my mouth.

"Well, only if you like this one," he said quickly, flipping through some pages on his clipboard. "And I'm sure you will, because we have a super fun day ahead of us! Our first activity is the ocean plunge — to wake us up for the morning!"

"Noah, we just got here..." I said. "What if we just take a few minutes to settle in?"

"Well, we have a full schedule..." he said. "But I guess the sunscreen will need to set for fifteen minutes anyway. Darn, I didn't plan for that."

And then, to my great discomfort, he took off his shirt and handed me the sunscreen.

"Could you get my back?"

For some reason, my heart started to race — and my stomach lurched. What was wrong with me? This was a beach. That's what people do at the beach.

I took the sunscreen and averted my eyes as I hurriedly applied the lotion, trying to ignore every part of his body that I touched.

"All set," I mumbled.

When I opened my eyes, I saw that half of his back was covered in white.

"Thanks!" he said, twisting and bending as he rubbed the rest into his chest and legs. "Want me to do you?"

I choked. "No!"

His eyebrows raised in concern. "You okay, doc?"

"Yes, sorry," I said, clearing my throat. "I'm feeling a bit car sick from the trip. I think I'm just going to read today."

He frowned. "You're not going to swim?"

"No," I said, staring intently at the sand by my feet. "But you go ahead."

He shrugged, put the sunscreen down, and ran toward the water.

As he disappeared into the waves, I let out a nervous, shaky breath.

This was definitely going to be our *last* company retreat.

For the rest of the day, we built sand castles, tossed frisbees, flew kites, and played a couple of games that Noah invented. My favorite was "Ocean Wars", where we had to dig a hole near the rising tide, and continually protect ourselves against the waves with walls of sand.

The ocean eventually defeated us, but we put up a pretty good fight.

By the time the sun started to set, I think I was actually having... fun. The whole retreat was also showcasing a lot of Noah's strengths that I had never seen (or noticed) in the office — especially his creativity and imagination. Kids were constantly coming up to us and asking to join in his games.

As we wandered back to our spots, I realized most of the beachgoers had cleared out.

"Looks like a storm is coming," I said, pointing to the dark clouds rolling in across the sea. "Ready to head back to the office?"

"We have to stay for the sunset and tell scary stories!" he protested. "It's the last item on the agenda."

"Noah, it's going to start pouring—"

"What if we move our stuff under the pier?" he said quickly, folding our chairs. "That way nothing gets wet."

I sighed and helped him pack up our things. We walked to the opposite side of the beach, which was now completely deserted, and made our way under the pier.

Moments later, there was a low rumble of thunder as rain began falling to the dock above us.

We spent the next hour or so telling scary stories, waiting for the storm to pass, but the rain was unrelenting. If there was ever a sunset, we didn't get to see it.

It was my turn to tell a story, but I'm not good at stuff like that, so I was basically just copying the plot of *The Shining*.

"And then, with his family hiding in the other room, he broke down the door with an axe—"

"Oh my god!" Noah shouted, lurching backwards.

"Oh, come on," I said. "It wasn't that scary."

But Noah wasn't looking at me.

He was looking *behind* me.

I spun around and jumped when I saw a young boy standing just inches away.

"Hey..." I said nervously. "You lost, little guy?"

The boy didn't answer, and his eyes were shut tight.

"Come on, let's get you back to your parents."

He just stood there, water dripping on him from the dock above.

There was a sudden flash of lightning, and that's when I saw an eerie message illuminated across the boy's shirt:

No See.

No Talk.

No Police.

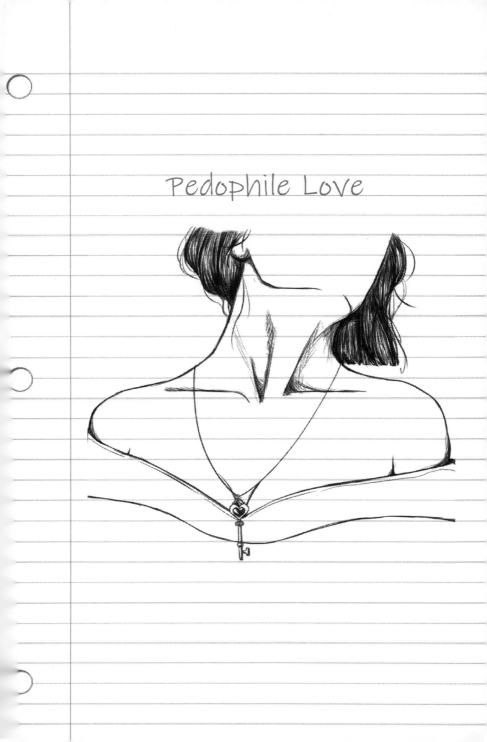

Pedophile Love

PART ONE

As I watched Arthur caress Sam's forearm, I shot them a glance — one that probably explained why half of my Yelp reviews described me as a 'judgmental jackass'.

"I know what you're thinking," said Arthur, who was at least three times older than Sam. "But I don't hurt kids anymore. I'm a reformed man now."

"Reformed?"

"That's right," he nodded proudly. "My spiritual guides helped me clear unprocessed energy in my sacral chakra. That's what was responsible for my dark urges."

"*Oh, good…*" I muttered. And here I was, worried that this would be another cliche Christian redemption story. But a New Age pedophile? That was… different.

"Sam, how old are you?" I asked.

"Eighteen," he said anxiously. "But I'm an old soul, you know? Other guys my age are into partying and stuff, but I like to drink tea and read."

"Oh, you drink *tea*?" I repeated. "Well, that changes everything."

Arthur looked at Sam, and then back to me.

"We were told that you work with… unique patients," said Arthur. "And we have a unique situation. But you're not—"

"What do you want me to say?" I interrupted him, putting my notebook away. "He's eighteen. You're — 100 or whatever. You're both consenting adults, you can do what you want."

"That's the problem!" said Arthur. "I don't know if he's consenting. And consent is very important to me now."

I slowly put my notebook down and looked back at them. "How can you not know if he's consenting?" I asked.

"He has a disease," said Arthur.

"It's not a disease!" Sam corrected him. "It's a mental illness."

"I guess that's where we disagree," said Arthur. "I view all mental problems as a disease of the spirit. I've done some energy work with Sam, and I sense a major blockage around his heart. Forgiveness is the key to opening the heart."

"Let me stop you right there," I said. "I'm a spiritual person too. And you know what I've found?"

Arthur looked at me, waiting for an answer.

"Abusive people *love* to use spirituality and forgiveness to manipulate their victims into accepting more abuse."

"That's not—"

"It's pretty clever, actually," I continued. "You can mistreat someone, and then make them feel *worse* by guilt-tripping and shaming them for the perfectly valid anger they carry. But real forgiveness does not require reconciliation or contact of any kind."

"I don't—"

"I'm done speaking with you," I said flatly, turning to face Sam. "Sam, have you been formally diagnosed with a mental illness?"

Arthur sunk bank into his chair and Sam nodded.

"Dissociative Identity Disorder," he said.

I raised my eyebrows and leaned forward. I had guessed this diagnosis for many of my past patients, and I had always been wrong.

"Are you receiving treatment here in the prison?" I asked.

I forgot to mention that — yeah, I'm in prison.

My patients got me thrown in here a while back. It took me a few months to adjust to my new life, but I've found my niche as the unofficial "prison psych". During lunch break, I hold sessions with inmates and help them sort through their problems. I already have a waiting list.

The problem is, the *actual* prison psychiatrist hates me. I've never even met or seen the woman, but she's already complained to the warden twice. Something about ethics.

"Yes, I'm being treated by Dr. Zhang."

"Look," I sighed. "I don't want to step on any toes here..."

"Please," Sam pleaded. "She just gives me pills and sends me away."

"Pills?" I said. "Anti-psychotics aren't typically recommended for DID."

"They're antidepressants and nightmare pills, for my PTSD."

I could already feel my analytical brain bursting with excitement. Sam had a co-morbid case of PTSD and DID, and something in him that felt attracted to a deeply dangerous man. This had to be the most interesting couple's therapy session of my life. Was I really willing to lose that, in order to keep the peace with some other therapist?

I bit my lip, and then spoke again.

"Can you tell me more about this consent issue?"

Sam nodded with relief. Arthur smiled too.

"I love him" said Sam, gazing into Arthur's eyes. "He's kind. He treats me well. He listens. He's sensual and passionate."

Arthur began rubbing Sam's arm again. They reminded me of newlyweds.

"So you two have... been together... physically?"

"Yeah, tons of times," said Sam.

"And you explicitly consented to those activities?"

"Yeah!" said Sam. "They were awesome."

"I'm sorry." I frowned. "I guess I'm just confused about the issue of consent."

"He changes," said Arthur.

Sam's ears went red and he looked down.

"What do you mean by 'changes'?"

"His disease," said Arthur darkly. "His other personality."

"We actually use the term *alter* instead of *personality*," I said. "So you're saying, you don't like this alter?"

"No, you've got it backwards." Arthur shook his head. "The

alter doesn't like *me*."

Sam's eyes watered with tears and he leaned into Arthur's arms. "I love you... I love you..." he whispered. "I'm sorry."

"There's nothing to apologize for," I said, growing more and more interested in their situation by the second. "Are there any particular events or activities that trigger the alter switching?"

"Yes," Arthur nodded. "His secret envelope."

"His secret... envelope?"

Sam looked at Arthur uncertainly.

"Go on," said Arthur encouragingly. "You can show him. I'll be here for you the whole time."

Sam nodded, reached into his pockets, and pulled out an envelope with no label.

"I have no idea what's in it," said Arthur. "He keeps it on him everywhere he goes. Refuses to show it to me — or anyone else."

"I can't remember what's in it," said Sam quietly. "All I know is that I'm the only person who's ever supposed to look."

"That's okay," I said. "But maybe if you shared it with me, I could—"

"No. Only me," said Sam, carefully opening the envelope. "Just, please don't listen to anything I say after this, okay?"

"Actually," I said hurriedly, realizing what was about to happen. "I'd really advise against triggering yourself in the middle of lunch—"

But before the words finished coming out of my mouth, Sam had opened the envelope and was staring wide-eyed at a polaroid photo.

At first, nothing happened.

But then Sam's pupils dilated into a look of pure terror.

"DON'T TOUCH ME!"

"It's okay, baby," Arthur rubbed his back. "I'm here for you—"

"DON'T!" Sam lurched away from him. "YOU'RE A BAD MAN!"

A few of the nearby inmates laughed, and the guards started walking our way.

"Let's all calm down," I whispered urgently. "Sam, can you just hand me the envelope?"

"PLEASE, HELP ME!" Sam begged, eyes streaming with tears. His face somehow looked younger, like a frightened child. *"Help me."*

Arthur tried one more time to comfort him, but Sam spat in his face and sprinted away, screaming as shoved the envelope into his pocket.

The guards chased him and tackled him to the ground.

"Do you see now?" said Arthur, standing up from the table. "I don't know which alter to believe — Does he love me? Does he fear me? Does he even consent to our relationship?"

At a loss for words, all I could do was stare as Arthur ran off to help Sam.

Five minutes ago, consent seemed like such a simple thing — yes or no. But what about a traumatized brain, where one part consents and another does not?

Were both alters speaking for Sam? Or was one of them more valid than the other?

Unfortunately, the answer seemed to live in Sam's pocket.

"I guess that's why they say it's never a good idea to get back together with your ex."

My cellmate, Tony, took a seat next to me at the lunch table.

"Ex?" I said. "What are you talking about?"

Tony adjusted his arm sling, even though his arm wasn't broken. He claimed it blocked mind-controlling chem trails from the sky.

"Arthur and Sam."

"What about them?" I pressed. "Did they have some sort of relationship before this?"

"Well," he said through a full mouth. "I wouldn't exactly call it a relationship."

"Why not?"

He looked up from his tray and raised his eyebrows.

"Because it was ten years ago, doc."

PART TWO

"You didn't think it was worth mentioning that you molested him as a child?"

Arthur and Sam both looked down.

"We didn't want you to treat us differently," Arthur mumbled.

"It *is* different," I said, shoving my lunch tray aside the next day. "It changes everything."

"But it was a decade ago!" said Arthur.

"Trauma doesn't have an expiration date," I snapped. "Every decision Sam makes today could be a result of that trauma."

"What do you mean?" Sam spoke up.

"Sam..." I softened my tone. "A young child does not have the emotional tools necessary to understand why a full-grown adult would harm them like that. And so often times, the body and mind put measures in place to protect them."

"What kind of measures?"

"Things to numb out the pain—"

"Well I didn't numb it out," he said confidently. "I can remember it, and it wasn't that bad."

"That's exactly what I'm talking about," I said. "Many trauma survivors can re-tell their stories in vivid detail, a hundred times over, but that doesn't mean the pain is gone."

"How can I possibly be carrying pain that I don't feel?" he asked.

"Because it's been split into another part of your body and mind," I said. "In this case, your alter."

Sam scoffed. "He's emotional. Unstable."

"He needs *help*," I said. "He was much younger. And he was terrified."

"Well then, we just need to get rid of him, right?"

"No," I said. "He's an important part of who you are. And we have to give him a chance to express himself. In a less stressful environment."

"Express himself?"

"Yes," I said. "When you're in a calm place, we can ask him to interact with us. It's likely going to be very uncomfortable, but I can teach you to become comfortable with discomfort. And then with enough time, we can integrate these parts of you — so that you can feel whole again, and able to trust your choices."

"So after that," Arthur spoke up. "If he still wants to be with me, then we know it's real consent?"

I shot him a nasty look. "Let's focus on Sam first here."

"It's a fair question," said Sam. "That's the whole reason we came to see you."

I sighed and rubbed my eyes.

"Sam, your ability to consent has been manipulated and distorted," I said. "There is a very high probability that Arthur groomed you as a child."

"Groomed?"

"Yes," I said. "Showering you with gifts and kindness to build trust. And then when he violated you, teaching you to blame and doubt yourself."

"I did no such—"

"Things like convincing you that you asked for it," I continued. "Or that your body's natural reactions to sexual stimulation were proof that you *liked* it."

"But—"

"Arthur, if you *actually* care for Sam," I said. "You'll happily support my meeting his alter. And you'll be grateful for his healing, whether or not he chooses to pursue this... relationship."

His eyes met mine. "Then let's do it."

"Sam?" I asked.

He nodded. "Okay."

"Wonderful," I said. "Now, when working with the mind and body, it's important that we ground ourselves. That means finding an environment or activity that helps us feel present in our body. Can you think of anything like that?"

"Well," he said nervously. "I've always liked to dance."

I gave him an encouraging smile.

"Then let's dance."

"You have thirty minutes," said the guard, standing by the broom closet. "Leave the radio. Keep it quiet and clean."

"What?" I said. "We're not—"

"Thank you," Arthur said to the guard. "The payment should clear tonight."

The guard opened the door and stepped aside.

"Good luck," Arthur whispered to Sam.

Sam nodded and entered the closet. I followed.

I picked up the radio from a nearby stool. It was one of those ancient ones, but it still turned on.

"Let me know when you hear something you like," I said to Sam as I turned the dial.

He shook his head a few times and said, "They're all too fast."

"Oh, I thought this was going to be a dance party," I said. "Are you looking for more of a slow song?"

"Yeah," he said with a laugh. "Before she passed, my mom and I used to waltz while we did the dishes after dinner. It's one of my favorite memories."

"That sounds really nice," I said, continuing to turn the dial.

"Perfect!" His eyes lit up as a staticky version of Elton John's *Your Song* played from the speaker.

I nodded and placed the radio back on the stool.

"Can we turn off the lights?" he asked. "I think there's enough light coming from the door."

I reached for the switch and flicked the lights off. He was

right — there was still plenty of light.

"My mom was taller than me," he said, inching closer to me. "So she would usually rest her arms on my shoulders."

I raised my eyebrows. "You want me to…?"

He nodded.

I hesitated for a moment, but then reminded myself that the whole goal here was to recreate the safe touch and environment that helped him feel grounded. So I gently draped my arms around his shoulders, ensuring a healthy distance between our bodies.

Sam reached out and placed his hands on my hips.

We began swaying softly to the song, and I saw his face break into a smile.

"I always wanted to dance like this at prom," he said. "Every time they played a slow song, it was all I could think about."

"Why didn't you?" I asked.

"I don't know." He shrugged. "After the whole thing with Arthur, I felt sort of… disconnected. More like an observer of the world, rather than a participant. Does that make sense?"

"That's a common reaction to trauma."

"I just feel like I missed out on so much of my life," he said quietly. "Dances… Friends… My first kiss — at least, a normal one."

For the next few minutes, we talked more about that "disconnected" feeling, and the things that Sam wished he hadn't missed.

Then he took one hand off my hip and reached into his pocket to take out his envelope.

"Okay, ready?"

"Yes," I said. "Are you feeling safe and comfortable? If not, we can—"

"I feel safe," he said confidently.

"Okay," I said. "And Sam, one more thing."

"Yeah?"

"You're likely going to feel intense sensations of shame, self-loathing, and self-doubt — persistent voices that tell you it's all your fault. That you're a liar."

He looked down. "What am I supposed to do if that happens?"

"I want you to *allow* those feelings," I said. "While also considering that they may not be true. Just observe and notice the sensations, but don't believe them."

He took a deep breath and nodded again.

Then he opened the envelope and looked at the photo inside.

Just like last time, he was calm for a moment.

And then his eyes went wide.

"Hey there," I said gently. "Stay with me, okay?"

Sam looked up and his eyes locked onto mine.

"You're safe here," I said. "You're safe."

His breathing became labored and fast, chest and shoulders raising sharply with every breath.

"My chest hurts," he whispered. "I can't breathe right."

"Try through your nose and belly," I said, doing it myself. "*In… and out…*"

He took a few breaths like that, keeping his eyes on mine every second — almost like he was afraid to look away.

Then he blurted out: "I'm a freak."

"That's not true," I said, tightening my hold on his shoulders. "Remember, you can stay with that feeling without *believing* it."

"But it *is* true," he protested, eyes burning. "I'm a sick freak. I wanted it."

"I want you to experiment with detaching from that voice," I said. "What if that voice isn't yours, but instead a voice from Arthur that you took on as your own?"

"How can I detach from it?" he stammered. "It's — It's coming from inside of me. It's who I am."

"No, it's not," I said firmly. "It's the voice of shame. The ultimate liar. Can you allow it to be there, without accepting it as truth?"

He bit down on his lip and squinted his eyes, a battle waging in his mind.

"Remember, you don't have to make it go away right now," I said. "All you need to do is *notice* this voice. And even as you try to do that — the voice might laugh at you, or ridicule you, or convince you that this is bullshit."

"It's doing all of that!" he cried.

"And all you need to do is *notice* those things," I said. "Just watch how hard that voice is putting up a fight — how hard it is trying to stay inside of you."

"But how do I make it stop?"

"Don't worry about that right now," I said. "Just stay with it. Stay with the pain. Become comfortable with discomfort, so that your alter doesn't need to take over and protect you."

He stared at me desperately, eyes haunted by years of untold wounding.

"You are a good person, Sam," I said softly, holding his gaze. "I promise, you are good."

His eyes filled with tears, and he buried his face in my chest. I held him, and we swayed in the dim light of the closet. Eventually, the music faded to static.

When our time was up, the door opened. But Arthur and the guard weren't anywhere in sight.

Instead, a short woman stood in the doorway, tilting her head with a pensive smile — one that lasted much longer than a normal smile.

"Doctor Peggy Zhang," she finally spoke, extending her hand to me. "I'm the prison psychiatrist."

I took a step away from Sam to shake her hand.

"Dr. Harper," I said. "It's nice to meet—"

"*Hmmm…*" She looked like she was lost in some sort of deep thought. "Our paths have finally crossed, Mr. Harper."

"*Doctor* Harper," I corrected her.

She gave me another head-tilt-smile. Then no one spoke for an uncomfortably long time.

"Please, come with me," said Dr. Zhang. "We need to talk about Sam."

"I'd just like a few more minutes with him," I said. "We made some really great progress—"

"*Hmmm*..." She smiled again and surveyed the room behind me. "Progress? In the broom closet? With an eighteen-year-old boy?"

"What? We were just—"

She let out another soft *hmmm*, which seemed to be her way of indicating that I should stop speaking.

"Come with me, Mr. Harper," she said. "There's something you need to know about Sam."

PART THREE

Dr. Zhang's office looked like the Buddha threw up inside of an Ashram.

Himalayan sea salt lamps illuminated statues of Indian deities around the room, and her shelves were lined with mainstream books on Eastern philosophy and positive thinking. Peaceful flute music played from the ceiling, complimented by the gentle trickling of mini waterfall-rocks around the office.

I sat across from Dr. Zhang, and we seemed to be locked in some sort of battle of silence. Neither of us had spoken a word since the moment we arrived.

But, predictably, my patience expired first.

"Is there something you wanted to talk about?" I asked.

Dr. Zhang tilted her head, smiled, and took two sips from a bottle of Kombucha. She wore a necklace with a dangling key, which sparkled in the dim light of the room.

"Look," I said. "I get it. You're one of those therapists who waits for the patient to start speaking first. But I don't even know why we're—"

"*Hmmm...*"

The sound came from her nostrils, and it always seemed to be accompanied by a deep look of reflection and contemplation.

"Mr. Harper," she said after a few moments. "Sam has indicated that he would prefer to pursue treatment with you."

"Oh, is that what this is about?" I laughed. "Listen, I don't want to step on any toes. I know you're the professional around here. I'm just trying to help. But I'll explain to him that you're still—"

"*Hmmm…*"

I did my best to conceal an irritable sigh. This was starting to become extremely annoying.

Dr. Zhang removed the key from her necklace and used it to unlock her desk drawer, pulling out a sealed folder.

Using a "*NAMASTE*"-inscribed letter opener, she cut through the seal and handed me a stack of papers.

"What are these?" I asked.

"They're Sam's files," she said. "I hope they help with your treatment."

"Wait, that's it?" I raised my eyebrows. "You're just going to — let me treat your patient?"

She tilted her head and smiled. "Mr. Harper, I hope we would never jeopardize a patient's wellbeing over some sort of imagined… turf war."

"No," I said, relieved. "No, of course not. Thank you."

"I would also encourage Sam to remain on Prazosin and Zoloft for his PTSD," she said. "However, he no longer seems interested in my advice."

"I can convince him," I said quickly. "The last thing he needs right now is an abrupt withdrawal from his medications."

She nodded and reached into her desk, handing me two orange bottles.

I frowned. "Won't I get in trouble for carrying prescription pills?"

"I've already spoken with the guards," she said. "I doubt you'll come across an inmate with an addiction to anti-depressants and blood pressure medications."

I laughed. "Fair enough."

She took another sip from her drink, locked the drawer, and then motioned for the guard outside the door to escort me back to my cell.

While we walked, I took a quick glance through the files, curious to learn more about Sam for our next lunch session. Dr. Zhang had definitely done her homework.

There were safe phrases:

Grounding words: darling day, morning sunshine, night star
Things to avoid:
Triggers rapid alter switch: fireflies, moonlight, satin sheets, secret envelope
And something very interesting that I hadn't even considered:
Ethan... 3rd alter...?

"Were you one of the Glade Farm boys?" Tony asked at lunch the next day.

"What's that?" Sam looked up from his tray.

"The pedo-ring." Tony lowered his voice. "Here in the prison."

"Alright," I said, raising my hand. "Let's take a break from the conspiracies and let Sam eat."

I had to admit, it was nice having Sam join us for lunch. Tony was friendly enough, but his conspiracies got on my nerves sometimes. Sam's skepticism made it a lot easier to tolerate him.

Sam had decided to take a break from Arthur to work on himself, which Arthur surprisingly agreed to (after consulting his tarot cards).

"Sam," I said, reaching into my pocket. "Dr. Zhang gave me your prescriptions, and I'd really recommend you continue with them."

Sam hesitated for a moment, then reached out his hand and took the pills from me.

"You think I need them?" he asked quietly.

"It's not a matter of need," I said. "Abruptly stopping any psychiatric drug could drastically worsen your mental health. If you'd like, I'd be happy to work on a taper plan with you."

He nodded and swallowed the pills with a sip of water.

We spent the next half hour joking around and entertaining Tony's conspiracies. This wasn't exactly how I imagined my life going, but they were good company, and friendships would probably be the best way to pass time around here.

Sam was looking sweaty and a bit agitated, so I encouraged him to drink more water.

"I think the Earth probably *is* flat," I said to Sam, giving him a quick wink as I pushed my water to him. "If you think about it, it really would be the easiest way for the government to —"

Suddenly his face went white as a ghost, and his eyes locked onto something behind me.

I turned around and saw Arthur enter the cafeteria with his two friends.

"It's okay," I comforted Sam. "He can't hurt you anymore."

Sam's breathing became stilted and rapid again.

I stood up to join him on the other side of the table.

"You're going to be okay," I said again, just like the broom closet.

He shook his head. "I feel so bad. Like my heart is a screaming fireball — but it can't get out of my chest."

"That's okay," I said. "Allow the fireball to be there."

"No, you don't GET IT!" he shouted.

I raised my eyebrows, taken aback. "Why don't we—"

"Something is wrong inside of my body!" he cried. "Feel my pulse!"

I touched two fingers to his neck, long enough to feel his heart racing well beyond any healthy rate.

"This is a normal reaction to a trigger—"

"DON'T TOUCH ME!" He spun around and bit my hand — hard.

"*What the hell,*" I muttered under my breath, shaking out my hand.

Sam had never been violent toward me. This was unlike any side I had seen to him. Was this the third alter that Dr. Zhang had warned about?

"Ethan?" I asked gently.

"What the FUCK are you talking about?" he said. "I'm SAM!"

At this point, the other inmates were starting to stare. It was only a matter of time before the guards intervened. So I hurriedly grabbed Dr. Zhang's notes from my pocket and scanned for the grounding safe words.

"*Darling day...*" I said soothingly. "*Morning sunshine...*"

His pupils dilated, and his eyes began to water.

"STOP IT!" he screamed. "THAT'S WHAT *HE* USED TO CALL ME!"

Then he reached into his pocket and took out the secret envelope.

"No!" I tried to stop him.

But I was too late.

Sam held out the polaroid in front of him for a few seconds. Then he threw it on the table, bolted up from his chair, and sprinted toward Arthur.

I ran after him, but everything happened so fast.

First, Sam pulled a knife from his pocket and drove it into Arthur's neck.

Then one of Arthur's friends took the knife out of his neck and stabbed Sam repeatedly in the chest.

"No!" I shouted as they scattered away.

"I'm sorry," whispered Sam, coughing up blood. "I don't... I don't know what happened to me."

I knelt down next to him. "You're fine. Just stay with me, okay?"

He coughed again and a tear fell down his cheek. "Am I going to die?"

"No." My heart sank. "Just think about Tony's funny conspiracies, okay?"

He shut his eyes. "Is there an afterlife, Dr. Harper?"

"Hey, come on." I shook him gently. "Keep your eyes open."

"I'm so afraid," he stammered. "Please, tell me if there's an afterlife?"

My eyes stung. "I — I think we're made of the same stuff as the stars."

"The stars?" he repeated.

"Yes," I said truthfully, trying to ignore the shouting guards approaching us. "I think we all have lessons to learn. Old energy and wounds to resolve. So we keep coming back until our work is done, and then we're infinite and free — just like the stars.

But it usually takes a few tries."

"A few tries?"

"Sure," I said. "Like, you've done all of this hard work to build boundaries and self-respect. So next time, your spirit will come armed with those wonderful skills."

He didn't respond.

"Hey, Sam, come on," I whispered. "Keep your eyes open."

Another tear ran down his face.

"Maybe next time, I'll come back with a little less pain in my heart."

There was a momentary glimmer of hope painted across his face, but Sam never opened his eyes again.

The guards pulled me away from Sam, shoving me into a line against the wall with several other prisoners.

"What the fuck happened here?"

"The kid charged!" said Arthur's friend. "All wide-eyed and crazy. Like he was fucking high or something."

High...

I thought for a second, then dug my hands into my pocket for Sam's remaining pills. Turning to conceal my hand, I opened the one labeled Zoloft (Sertraline) and sprinkled a pill onto my palm. I leaned in close and examined the letters on it:

CHX 4.0

"*Chantix?*" I whispered. "*What the fuck?*"

Chantix was a smoking cessation pill, well-known for agitating the mind and having an insanely high rate of violent and suicidal reactions — 18 times higher than the average pharmaceutical drug. And 4mg was eight times higher than the standard dose.

Heart racing, I unscrewed the cap from the Prazosin — a blood pressure medication that can also mitigate nightmares for patients suffering from PTSD.

But once again, this pill looked nothing like the dual-colored capsule that Prazosin typically comes in. It was just a solid white pill, and there was no label.

What the hell had I given Sam?

"WHOSE SHIV IS THIS?" The guard shouted, marching down the line with the knife in his hand. "TALK. NOW."

My eyes went wide when I saw it wasn't a knife at all.

It was a letter opener — inscribed with the the word "*NAMASTE*".

"That would be mine," came a familiar voice.

I felt my entire body tense up when I saw Dr. Zhang walking toward us.

"*Hmmm...*" She bent down and gazed at Sam. Then she stood up and slowly walked over to me. "Mr. Harper, it would seem that I made a mistake leaving him in your care."

"You fucking bitch—" I lunged forward to choke her, but the guards knocked me down immediately.

"Mr. Harper—"

"You're a fucking psychopath! Poisoning a traumatized kid, sending his dopamine levels to the moon and back, giving him a weapon, using his triggers against him—"

"*Hmmm...*" She lowered herself to my level. "Mr. Harper, your little tantrums may have worked outside of these walls, but I would prefer that we communicate like adults."

She stood up.

"Guards, I believe Mr. Harper took my letter opener when he was in my office yesterday," she said. "Sam O'Dell suffered from Multiple Personality Disorder, and it would seem that one of his personalities was prone to violence—"

"HOLLYWOOD BULLSHIT," I spat. "It's called Dissociative Identity Disorder, and alters are rarely ever dangerous. They're far more likely to be victims than perpetrators. Sam was provoked and drugged—"

"*Hmmm...*" Dr. Zhang tilted her head and smiled sadly. "I don't wish to point fingers, Mr. Harper, but wasn't Mr. O'Dell *your* responsibility? Did you not ask to take over his care? So if he was provoked and drugged, as you claim, would that not implicate *you* as the primary suspect?"

I tried to take a deep breath, but my lungs didn't seem to fill with air.

"Guards, please search Mr. Harper's pockets."

They pinned me to the ground and found the two bottles. After handing them to Dr. Zhang, she leaned down again and whispered, "Where is the envelope?"

"What?" I said, accidentally eyeing our lunch table. "I don't have it."

She tilted her head again. "Guards, search that table."

They did as she said, and I groaned when they returned with Sam's secret envelope.

"Very good," she said, turning to face everyone else. "Now, it would seem that Mr. Harper has taken up the very same type of unethical therapy practices that landed him in jail to begin with. Unable to help himself, he convinces others to let him help them. But now we have seen what kind of *help* he offers."

"Oh, for fuck's sake—"

"I suspect Mr. Harper may be suffering from Narcissistic Personality Disorder," she continued. "And I look forward to treating him when he returns from his time in solitary confinement."

"What! I didn't—"

"*Hmmm...*" she said, pacing along the row of inmates. "I imagine 8 hours should give Mr. Harper ample time to reflect on the dangers of his private practice."

Before I could say another word, the guards grabbed me and marched me out of the lunchroom.

I turned around one last time and stared in disbelief at Dr. Zhang.

She simply tilted her head, smiled, and slipped the envelope into her pocket.

———————————————//———————————————

I returned to my cell that night and tried to keep quiet to avoid waking Tony. But he wasn't asleep.

"Doc, you're back," he said. "How was the SHU?"

"It was great," I grumbled. "I'm a changed man."

"I was worried you were CIA." He sat up from his bed and lifted his arm sling. "But you stood up to Zhang. No one does that. Not even COINTELPRO."

"Tony, I don't have time for conspiracies tonight," I said, pulling myself up to the top bunk. "I need to sleep."

"Doc," he said. "You don't have to believe everything I say, but I swiped Sam's photo. Kids are in danger."

I froze. "That's not possible. I saw Zhang take the envelope."

"Well," he said. "I took what was inside. Will you just take a look?"

I stepped off the ladder, curiosity getting the better of me.

Tony handed me the photograph that had triggered Sam multiple times.

I took one look and dropped it on the ground. "Jesus, Tony! That's — it's child porn."

It was exactly what I expected. Arthur, and a much younger Sam.

"Grow up, Doc," he said. "This isn't about you. That kid was hurting."

"What do you want me to do?" I said, exasperated. "Sam is dead. There's nothing I can do—"

"Pick up the photo," said Tony. "Maybe there are other kids you can help."

I shook my head and picked up the picture from the ground.

"What am I supposed to be seeing?" I asked.

"Turn it around," said Tony.

I did as he said, and felt my heart sink as I read the Sharpie-scrawled label on the back:

Glade Farm Boy #93

End of Patient File: The Wolf

Dr. Harper Therapy Company Retreat

The Wolf

"Noah, call 911."

"But his shirt says *No Police*."

I stared at him incredulously.

"Oh — right," he said, reaching into his pocket. "I'll call now. Should you... Check his vitals?"

"I'm not a nurse," I snapped. "I'll try and talk with him."

He nodded and took out his phone.

While he talked to the police, I bent down to the kid's level. I've never been great with younger kids — let alone mysterious missing children on the beach.

"Are you able to hear me?" I asked awkwardly.

His eyes remained clamped shut.

"You don't need to respond," I continued. "I just want to tell you that we're calling the police, and everything's going to be okay."

He bowed his head down.

"Can you tell me your name?" I asked.

He didn't reply to that question, or to any of my others. It was starting to feel like an interrogation.

Noah finished his call. "They're on the way!"

"Great." I stood up, relieved.

"How are things going over here?" he asked quietly

"He's not talking at all," I said. "I wonder if he might

have some variation of Avoidant Personality Disorder—"

"Doc!" Noah interrupted me. "Not everything needs to be a diagnosis."

"I'm a psychiatrist!"

"Well, he's not a patient," said Noah protectively, sitting down in the sand next to the boy. "He's a *cool kid*. And what do cool kids like?"

"What are you talking about—"

"*Shhh...*" Noah raised his hand at me, turning all of his attention to the boy. "Cool kids like... Broccoli!"

The boy's eyes remained closed, but he raised his eyebrows. That was already more progress that I had made.

"And cool kids like... brushing their teeth!" Noah made a fake gargling sound and spat on the ground.

The boy let out a tiny, but unmistakable giggle.

"Nah, I'm just kidding." Noah laughed too. "Cool kids like *adventures*, right? Do you want to go on a magical adventure with us? I can teach you spells and potions!"

The boy took a deep breath, then nodded.

Noah grabbed a twig from the sand and extended it to the boy.

"Here is your wand, brave wizard," he said seriously. "Will you join me on this quest?"

I watched in disbelief as the boy opened his eyes, blinked a few times, then reached forward to accept the twig.

"*How the hell...*" I muttered under my breath.

"And do you have a name, young wizard?"

He nodded. "James."

"It's nice to meet you, James!" Noah grabbed two more sticks for us. "For your first task, you must make a very important decision. Do we go through the ancient forest, climb the mystical mountains, or fly into the night sky?"

James held the wand in front of him.

"Fly."

"The best choice," said Noah. "There's a hot air balloon right over here. Let's all climb in!"

The three of us walked a few paces to the right as Noah welcomed us onto the imaginary balloon.

"Watch your feet!"

I stared at him as I slowly stepped to his side.

"Can you light the balloon for us?" Noah asked James. "The spell is *FIREBALL!*"

James nodded excitedly. Then he twirled the stick in the air and said, "Fireball!"

"*FOOM!*" said Noah, making an exploding motion with his arms. "Wow, you're a very powerful wizard."

James beamed.

"We're taking off!" said Noah, leaning over the non-existent edge. "Look at the stars all around us."

James stood next to him and looked out over the sky.

"I see a cloud over there," Noah pointed into the distance. "Should we see if anyone lives there?"

James nodded, so Noah grabbed an imaginary steering wheel and took us to the cloud.

"Looks like there's something on the cloud," said Noah. "What is that?"

James leaned forward, squinted, and then his eyes went wide.

"It's a wolf."

Noah gasped. "A wolf, of course! And it just hopped onto our balloon. What does it want?"

"He wants to take me," said James, breathing more rapidly. "He says I should come live on the cloud with him."

"Well, we can't have that," said Noah, holding out his wand. "Don't worry, we won't let him take you. Everyone, ready your wands."

James held out his wand.

"Mr. Wolf," said Noah. "Please leave us alone."

Then he looked at me expectantly.

"Oh — right," I said stiffly, holding out the stick. "Yes, leave us alone."

"He doesn't want to," said James quickly. "He says I'll be much happier there. He says there are hundreds of other boys who live on the cloud, and we can all be friends."

"Hundreds!" exclaimed Noah. "Wow, that's a lot."

"The wolf is a collector," said James. "He collects boys like me for the cloud. He gives us presents and lets us eat candy all day, but we can't tell anyone what happens at night."

I suddenly felt chills run down my spine. There was something horribly wrong with James' contributions to the story.

"*Noah,*" I whispered. "*Ask him if there are any other animals on the cloud.*"

Noah raised his eyebrows, then turned to James. "Are there any other animals on the cloud? Or just the wolf?"

"Yes," said James, peering into the distance. "There are four more animals. And they are all very bad. This cloud is bad."

Noah looked at me nervously, then turned back to James.

"So the wolf collects little boys for the cloud..." said Noah quietly. "What do the other animals do?"

HIV Infections

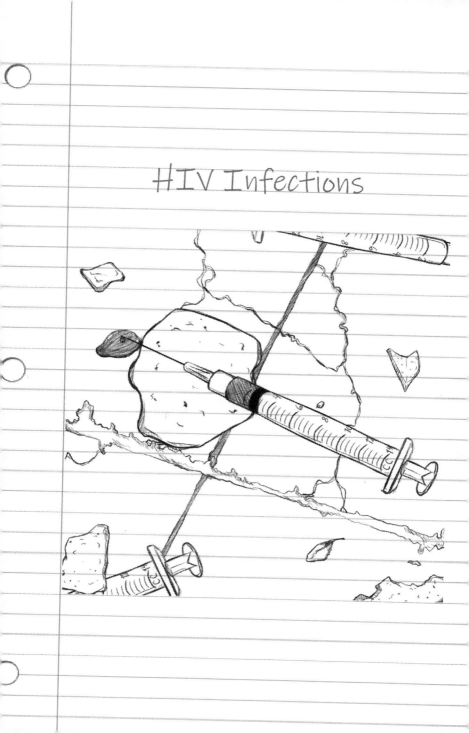

HIV Infections

PART ONE

"They *wanted* it," said Don. "That's what you're not understanding."

"Why would someone *want* to get HIV?" I asked.

The weather was finally nice enough for us to get some time outside, so we were sitting on the bleachers and tossing a baseball back and forth.

"Dr. Harper, you ever tried meth?"

"No," I said. "But—"

"Okay then. That's the problem," he said simply. "You don't get what kind of fucked up stuff it makes you feel."

"Meth makes people want to get HIV?" I said skeptically.

"It makes you want things you never knew you wanted…" He sounded like he was talking about a long-lost lover. "Imagine your most sketchy sexual fantasies, then multiply that by a million."

Don was a young man who had actually sought help from me before my trial, but I had gotten caught up with other clients.

"How is receiving an STD a sexual fantasy?"

"Because, you have a part of them inside of you forever," he said. "Plus, then you don't have to deal with the anxiety of getting HIV anymore."

I took a long look at him, trying to figure out if he was telling the truth.

"So…" I said. "You're telling me… All eight of the men who accused you of infecting them with HIV — they wanted it at the time?"

"Yes," he said. "We had conversion parties. They used the needle right after me, just to increase their odds. Then they would lay there like pigs, ready to take my—"

"Okay." I raised my hand. "I get it. So what changed their mind?"

"They got sober," he said with a laugh. "There's the first mistake. Without meth, they got ashamed of their inner slut and blamed it on me."

"What about you?" I asked. "Are you still using, after what it's done to your life?"

He looked at me and grinned.

"You've never let yourself lose control, have you?"

I cleared my throat. "This isn't about me."

"Well, this is the same kind of judgy bullshit that I'd expect from a control freak."

"I'm not judging!" I protested. "I'm just trying to understand what happened, so I can help you."

"And I'm telling you, these guys contacted *me* on Grindr. They saw the capital T for Tina. They saw I was positive. They were bug chasers."

"Bug chasers?"

"Dudes who *want* HIV," he said. "To get it over with. That way they don't have to worry about it anymore."

As we continued talking, I noticed Don's cellmate eyeing us from the nearby tables. As soon as I made eye contact with him, he looked away.

"Why is your cellmate watching us?"

I had already gotten into trouble for my unofficial therapy sessions, and I didn't want to draw any more unnecessary attention to myself.

"I don't know." Don shrugged. "He's probably jealous."

"Jealous?"

"Probably thinks you and I are gonna fuck," he said, leaning closer to me. "You wanna fuck?"

"Come on, Don—"

"I'd be down." He slowly ran his tongue across his lower lip. "Something about the way you're so fucking hostile and rigid.

Just makes me want to roll you over and watch you writhe."

I felt my face flush, losing any upper-hand I may have had in our dynamic.

"Look at you, going all red…" Don laughed. "Jesus, it's like you've never fucked another dude before."

My heart raced as I tried to come up with a way to change the topic. "We need to—"

"Holy shit." He leaned forward. "You're a virgin!"

"Don—"

"What, are you saving yourself for prison marriage?" he asked. "Fuck, Harper, I'm gonna teach you how to have fun."

He reached into his pocket and pulled out a syringe.

"No!" I whispered, looking around anxiously. "Put that away!"

"Relax, Harper."

As I tried to shield us from the view of any guards, he prepared the needle and stuck it in his arm.

He took a deep breath in, and then let out a loud moan of pleasure.

"Now you."

He held out the syringe to me, and I quickly saw it was red with his blood.

"No." I shook my head, sliding a few inches away from him. "Absolutely not."

"Suit yourself." He shrugged. "Purity princess."

"This isn't about purity," I said, trying to regain control of the conversation. "It's about health and happiness. Don, don't you think there's a chance you're using sex and drugs to escape from some deeper issues?"

He frowned. "Like what?"

"I don't know," I said. "That's why I'm here. To learn more about you and your life."

"*Woo!*" His entire body shivered. "Okay, what do you want to know? I'm an open book."

"Are your mom and dad still in the picture?"

Therapy with an addict under the influence was about as effective as punching a brick wall, but at the very least I could try to understand how his current state of mind led to such reckless behavior.

"They kicked me out when I was a teenager."

"Because of your sexuality?" I asked.

"Yeah," he said. "The tragic gay boy cliche."

"Did that rejection hurt?" I asked. "From the people who are supposed to love you unconditionally?"

"I don't know," he said. "I didn't have time to think much about it. Had to find housing, money, all that."

"That's a lot to face at such a young age," I said gently. "No wonder you never had a chance to process the rejection."

His eyes met mine for a few moments, frenzied and dilated. And then, to my horror, he stuck his hand down his pants.

"What are you—"

But before I could protest any further, he covered my mouth with his other hand.

"I'm so fucking hot for you right now."

I squirmed to get away, but he was much stronger than me. I let out a muffled scream and desperately scanned the prison yard around us. Don's cellmate was the only one paying us any attention. I stared at him, eyes pleading — but he turned away.

"*You want this...*" Don whispered into my ear. "*You want this.*"

And seconds later, that's when I felt it.

The sting of a needle in my arm.

PART TWO

I waited inside of the infirmary while the doctor ran some tests, anxiously tapping my foot against the ground.

I tried to stay calm, reminding myself that the risk of contracting HIV — even through needle sharing — was relatively low. And I still didn't feel any sort of high from the incident, which hopefully meant that it didn't even make it into my bloodstream.

Finally, the doctor walked back into the room.

"I didn't find any methamphetamines in the syringe," he said. "In fact, the only substance in the tube was Mr. Halverson's blood — filled to the brim."

"He injected me with his... blood?" I repeated.

"It seems that way," said the doctor. "Now, given that Mr. Halverson has a high viral load, this poses a significant risk for transmission."

My heart started to pound. "I thought the odds were less than 1%."

"That's for sexual intercourse and needle sharing," he said. "This is a lot more like a blood transfusion."

I swallowed. "And what are the rates for that?"

"92%."

My whole body went numb and cold. It was some strange combination of helplessness, terror, and shame.

I had seen friends go through this — the panicked calls after a drunken night of unprotected sex. I guess I just thought I was immune from the problem, given my... solitary lifestyle.

My ears rang as the doctor's voice droned on in the distance.

"We need to get you started on post-exposure prophylaxis. If taken within 72 hours, it can effectively prevent HIV infection—"

"I'm a gay psychiatrist," I said impatiently, snapping back to reality. "I know what PEP is."

"I see..." He raised his eyebrows. "Well, if you're comfortable with the treatment and potential side effects, I'd recommend we get started immediately."

"Agreed."

"Excellent," he said, walking over to the door. "Now, because this involved a high-risk LGBTQ encounter, our psychiatrist will complete the evaluation and prescription."

"Oh, you've got to be fucking kidding—"

But I didn't even get a chance to finish my sentence, before I was interrupted by a familiar sound at the door.

"*Hmmm...*"

"Mr. Harper," she said. "I didn't expect to see you again so soon."

Dr. Zhang sat across from me in her office, holding two prescription bottles.

I bit my tongue, determined to remain polite, since my life was — quite literally — in her hands.

"Now..." She crossed her legs. "I just have a few questions before we get you started on treatment."

"Sure," I said pleasantly. "Anything."

"That's wonderful," she said with a smile. "Now, in addition to PEP, you may be aware of a medication called PrEP which can protect you from future exposures. Do you plan to continue engaging in these high-risk activities?"

"Oh," I said with a laugh. "This wasn't sex or drugs. He attacked me—"

"*Hmmm...*"

I took a deep breath and forced a smile. "Yes?"

"Well..." She tilted her head. "I can't help but wonder how you'll ever get better, if you continue to view yourself as a *victim* of these events?"

"I don't see myself as a victim," I protested. "It's just what happened—"

"*Hmmm…*"

I took another deep breath, but this one felt much less relaxing. "*Yes?*"

"Mr. Harper, you seem to find yourself in a lot of these situations where unfair things just *happen* to you." She smiled sadly. "And at some point, I can't help but wonder if it's time to notice the common denominator?"

I closed my eyes for a moment, then looked at the prescription bottles in her hands. That was all that mattered.

"You're right," I said. "I tend to take on dangerous projects so I can play the hero. Then when it blows up in my face, I feel victimized and betrayed."

She gazed at me silently for a few seconds. I could hear her Buddha clock ticking from the wall as she tried to read my mind.

Every tick was a reminder that PEP became less effective by the second.

Tick. Tick.

"Mr. Harper…" She took a sip from her Kombucha. "Could you tell me more about your affinity for younger men?"

I accidentally let out another small laugh. "What?"

"Well," she said. "Between this STI from Don—"

"He stabbed me with a needle."

"And your time with Sam in the broom closet—"

"It was a grounding exercise!"

"And your missing assistant…"

I froze. "What did you say?"

She smiled. "Your assistant. He was all over the news. Noah, right?"

I gritted my teeth.

"Did you care for him?" she asked. "Or were you merely using him to satisfy your more… primal urges?"

Unfortunately no amount of deep breathing seemed to help me relax anymore. But even as my heart began to race, those bottles in her hand managed to keep me from exploding.

Tick. Tick.

"I did care for him," I said quietly. "And I still do."

She studied me for a moment. "That's very nice to hear, Mr.

Harper."

"Thanks," I mumbled.

She leaned forward and put the bottles on the coffee table between us.

"Now," she said. "As you know, every second counts with PEP. The sooner you take it, the better. The first 48 hours are most effective, but it has been shown to work up to 72 hours."

I let out a huge sigh of relief and leaned forward. "I'll start right away."

"*Hmmm...*"

I hesitated, hands just inches away from the pills. "Yes?"

"Mr. Harper, we seem to have a funny situation."

I raised my eyebrows. "How is this funny?"

"Well," she said with a smile. "We both have something that the other person wants."

"What do you mean?" I said, heart pounding. "What do you want from me?"

She tilted her head.

Tick. Tick.

I thought for a moment, then realized — Sam's photo.

I had hidden it somewhere safe. It was the only evidence of the possible pedophile ring. I couldn't just give it back to her, especially if she was somehow involved.

"I don't have the photo," I said. "I swear."

She smiled again. "*Hmmm...*"

"Really, I don't," I said. "Please, you have to believe—"

"Mr. Harper," she interrupted me. "Assuming Noah is found some day, how do you think he would react to the news of your HIV status?"

I bit my lip.

"Surely, losing him can't be worth a silly little photo."

I finally realized that this wasn't a prescription. It was a negotiation. And now I had to make a choice between protecting my own health, and protecting a polaroid.

Tick. Tick.

My brain raced as it tried to analyze every possible outcome.

Despite Dr. Zhang's attempts to weaponize and stigmatize

HIV, it was actually highly treatable these days. Millions of people lived normal, happy lives with it. But was it worth protecting a single piece of evidence? The truth was, I had no proof that the photo was evidence of *anything*. Maybe there really were hundreds of children in danger. Or maybe it was just paranoid ramblings from my cellmate.

I listened intently as the inner debate carried on — heart versus mind.

My heart held onto the possibility of kids being hurt, and the far-fetched hope of obtaining PEP from other inmates. But my brain made much more logical arguments. Why should I martyr myself for a photo? If there really was a pedophile ring, surely there would be more opportunities to find evidence down the line.

Finally, I leaned forward and took the pills from the table.

She smiled. "A good choice, Mr. Harper. Now, the photo?"

I stood up, walked past her chair, and dropped the pills in her lap.

"Mr. Harper..." she said, standing up. "Don't be irrational. Without PEP, you'll almost certainly be infected with HIV — and all for something as insignificant as a photo?"

I turned to face her.

"Here's what I think." I leaned in close, so our eyes were just inches apart. "In all my life, I've never seen someone so desperate for a polaroid that they threaten a person with a life-threatening illness. So by my estimates, the photo is *pretty fucking significant*."

Dr. Zhang stared back at me. No smile. No head tilt. No patronizing hum.

I got the feeling I had just made a horrible mistake, but it was too late to turn back now. Heart racing, I stepped around her and knocked firmly on the door.

As I waited for the guard, the uncomfortable silence in the room was broken only by the Buddha clock on her wall.

Tick. Tick.

PART THREE

"I need your help."

I was surprised to see Don's cellmate, Bernard, slide down next to me at the lunch table.

"Yeah, like you helped me yesterday?" I grumbled.

"Would you just listen to me?" said Bernard. "I'm his sponsor, and I think he's in danger."

I raised my eyebrows. "Sponsor, like for AA?"

"Yes," he said. "I've been sober for thirty-two years."

"Congratulations," I said, loosening up a bit. "That's really great."

Bernard was an older man, but he still looked like he could knock the crap out of most of the guys here.

"The 12th Step is all about helping others achieve sobriety," he said. "That's why I took Don under my wing. But Jesus, that kid tests me."

"He's resisting the step work?"

"I've tried everything," he said, frustrated. "I even requested our living arrangement — so I could be more involved in his recovery."

"You weren't worried that he might try to infect you?"

"No, I'm guided by God," said Bernard simply. "And before I changed cells, I asked the doctor for some emergency meds — the ones you can take after an exposure. I carry 'em with me all the time."

"You have PEP?" My eyes went wide.

"Yeah, probably the same stuff they gave you."

I shook my head. "They didn't give it to me."

"What?" he exclaimed. "Why the hell not?"

"It's a long story," I said quickly. "Listen, can I borrow your meds? I promise, I'll get you more. But I only have 48 hours left to start treatment — I already lost a day."

"Sure," he said, reaching into his pocket. "Here."

My heart soared when I saw the two bottles. I had been desperately asking other inmates to help me, but HIV meds weren't really the kind of drugs floating around the prison black market.

"Thank you," I said, sprinkling a pill from each bottle into my hand.

Paranoid from Dr. Zhang's last stunt, I studied both pills to ensure their authenticity. The larger blue oval pill was inscribed with Truvada's signature "Gilead 701". The other was a tiny circular yellow pill with "50" stamped on one side. It was Tivicay.

A perfectly safe and effective PEP regimen.

I let out a huge sigh of relief and swallowed the two pills with a swig of water.

"Is it okay if I keep these?" I asked Bernard, holding up the bottles. "I've got to take them every day for a month, otherwise they won't work."

"Be my guest," he said. "Now, are you going to help *me*?"

I looked up, remembering that everything in here was a negotiation.

"Yes, of course," I said. "What do you need?"

"I'm with that kid *every* second of *every* day, and somehow he still manages to get high." Bernard moved closer to me. "Someone in here is dealing to Don, and I'm going to stop them."

"I don't know who," I said quickly. "I swear if I did, I would tell you."

"I think you *do* know, Dr. Harper," he said. "But you just don't know that you know."

"What?" I screwed up my face. "What does that even mean?"

"The other day, after that shit-show with Sam and Arthur, Don came back to our cell in a drug-induced frenzy. Rambling on about how he had to do something horrible, or his dealer would cut him off."

"Wait, his dealer told him to…?"

"Prick you with a dirty needle," said Bernard. "That's right."

"What!" I said. "Who the hell would want that?"

"That's exactly what I want to know," he said, lowering his voice. "Dr. Harper, do you have any enemies in here? Someone who could somehow… benefit… from you being infected?"

I thought for a moment, and then it finally all clicked.

The attack. The PEP negotiation. The photo demands.

This wasn't some sort of an unlucky coincidence. It was an orchestrated plan.

"Dr. Zhang," I said quietly. "She's the dealer."

He raised his eyebrows. "The psych doctor?"

"Yes," I said. "She's had it out for me since the day I got here. And now she's withholding PEP because she wants something from me."

"Christ…" he muttered. "I've heard stories about the woman, but I always thought they were urban legends."

We both sat there in silence for a while. Then he stood up from the table with his tray.

"Wait, where are you going?" I asked.

"To talk with Zhang."

"What?" I stood up too. "No, it's too dangerous."

"Don't worry." He walked over to the trash. "I won't mention you."

"No, I mean it's dangerous for you!" I trailed after him. "You don't want to get on her bad side."

He leaned against the garbage can and looked at me.

"Dr. Harper, do you know the serenity prayer?"

"Yes," I said.

He recited it for me anyway. *"God, grant me the serenity to accept the things I cannot change, the courage to change the things I can—"*

"And the wisdom to know the difference," I finished impatiently. "What does that have to do with anything?"

"In this case," he said, "God has granted me courage, because this is something I *can* change. Someone is intentionally hindering my sponsee's progress, and I have a chance to help him."

"But—"

"Dr. Harper, I've been here a lot longer than you," he said, taking his leave. "I can take care of myself."

As Bernard walked away, I bit my lip and got the sinking sensation that we'd never talk again.

In the evenings, Tony would work on his crossword puzzle while I wrote in my journal. It was a peaceful routine, and it gave us both a break from bickering about conspiracies.

But tonight, our quiet time was interrupted by the blaring prison alarm.

Tony and I both jumped from our beds and ran to the cell door as the inmates around us shouted and hollered.

Guards rushed across the way — to Bernard and Don's cell.

Minutes later, my heart sank when I saw them wheel a body out on a stretcher.

"The monster strikes again," Tony muttered, nursing his anti-mind-control arm sling.

"I warned him," I said. "I told him this would happen."

"Don't blame yourself," said Tony. "Same thing happened to his past four cellmates. Real shame though. He was young — had his whole life ahead of him."

I frowned, and then realized we seemed to be talking about a different 'he'.

"Wait a minute," I said. "Who do you think is on that stretcher? Bernard or Don?"

"The kid, of course."

"What?" I said. "No, it has to be Bernard. This afternoon, he was going to take a stand against Dr. Zhang for drugging Don."

Tony snorted. "I'm sure he didn't need Zhang's help to drug a kid."

"What are you talking about?" I walked over to the bed. "Bernard is his sponsor — 32 years sober."

"He may be sober," said Tony. "But he's the biggest dealer

in here."

"Dealer?"

"Well, every one of his cellmates ends up hooked on heroin, opiates, or meth. Then a month later, they have a *cardiac issue*. You do the math."

I shook my head. "It doesn't make any sense. Bernard helped me. He gave me HIV meds after Don attacked me."

Tony looked up from his crossword darkly. "If you accepted drugs from Bernard, you should expect to pay a heavy price. I'd flush them. Now."

"I can't!" I protested. "I'm in the final 24-hour window. If I miss tomorrow's dose, they'll be completely useless."

"Doc, HIV should be the least of your concerns right now," he said. "You're in business with a chemical assassin."

"Business?" I repeated incredulously. "Even if you're right, what the hell could Bernard possibly want from me?"

With a warning in his eyes, Tony shot a glance at the cell door and looked back at his puzzle.

I spun around and saw Bernard standing there next to two guards, and—

"*Hmmm…*"

I swallowed nervously as Dr. Zhang peered through the bars.

"Mr. Harper…" she said. "Bernard here tells us that you took his prescription."

"What? He—"

"Guards, toss the cell."

They did as she said, immediately finding the PEP bottles under my pillow.

"Mr. Harper…" She tilted her head sadly, holding the bottles out to me. "Stealing pills? Again?"

"*Please,*" I whispered.

"I thought you seemed unusually confident in my office yesterday," she said. "But that was only because you were planning to *cheat*."

"Please," I said again. "I'll do anything."

"*Hmmm…*" She smiled and lowered her voice. "The photo?"

I bit my lip and closed my eyes.

"I'm disappointed," she said, wandering over to the toilet. "I'm curious to see if you change your mind in a place where *cheating* isn't an option."

"No—" I protested.

"Guards, please escort Mr. Harper to solitary."

As they cuffed my hands, Dr. Zhang slowly began sprinkling the PEP into the toilet.

"24 hours should give him ample time to reflect on the... *urgency*... of his situation."

End of Patient File: The Bumble Bee

Dr. Harper Therapy Company Retreat

The Bumble Bee

"I don't want to talk about the other animals," said James.

"That's okay!" said Noah quickly. "We're leaving the cloud right now. We're going to fly over the ocean now, and we're turning on the invisibility shield, so none of the animals can find us."

"Wait," I said. "But shouldn't we learn more—"

"Doc," whispered Noah. "He's upset. Let's just help him relax until the police get here."

I sighed and nodded. He was probably right, but I really wanted to learn more.

"This is a special ocean that glows in the dark!" Noah turned back to James. "We're the only creatures up here. Just us, and the waves crashing below."

James took a deep breath and closed his eyes.

"Do you want to rest?" asked Noah. "This is a great time to sleep. Floating up here, safe and sound, invisible above the sea. Here, I'll make you a bed in the stars."

As I watched Noah lay out our damp towels, I couldn't help but notice that there was something so caring and purposeful about the way he created this imaginary world for the boy.

"This is a magical bed," said Noah to James. "Because when you look into the pillow, you can see the whole ocean sparkle below you. It's like a light show — the waves, the water, the fish — everything is dancing with color!"

James hurried over to the towels and lay down face-first into the pillow.

"How did you learn how to do this?" I whispered to Noah.

He tilted his head. "Learn what?"

"The balloon, the magic, the ocean — all of it," I said. "Is it some kind of grounding exercise?"

"Hmm, I don't know." He shrugged. "I just like telling stories, and it seemed like he might need one."

"Oh," I said quietly. "Well, you're really good at it."

His face lit up and he moved a bit closer to me. "Thanks, doc!"

In that moment, even though I'm the most unimaginative person on the planet, I truly felt that we were leaning over the edge of a balloon together, looking out across the glowing ocean.

———————————— // ————————————

Minutes later, James started screaming.

"Are you okay?" Noah hurried over and helped him up from the bed.

"The animals found us," he sobbed. "The bumble bee stung me."

"Oh no!" said Noah, searching for the mark. "Can you show me where?"

James pointed to the inside of his left arm.

I peered closer and was horrified to see red marks and scars all over — like a long-time intravenous drug user.

That definitely wasn't from a bee.

"Why did it sting you?" I asked.

James looked at me nervously, and then turned to Noah.

Noah nodded, implying that it was okay to answer me.

"He stings us for three reasons." James' voice was barely audible. "The first reason is to put us to sleep."

"What about the second reason?" I pressed.

He hung his head. "To make us feel good when we do the bad thing."

Noah and I glanced at each other uneasily.

"And the third reason?"

Noah stepped between us. "You don't have to—"

"Please," I said to both of them. "Tell us the third reason, so we can help you."

James winced, eyes burning red.

"When boys say no, the bee puts them to sleep."

Before I could ask for clarification, he added one more word:

"Forever."

Unusual Addiction

Unusual Addiction

In most social interactions, a certain degree of mirroring is healthy and expected. From a young age, we learn to take on the subtle tones, gestures, and inflections of the people around us. It's actually a sign of well-developed empathy, and it tends to result in stronger interpersonal connections.

Mirroring can become troublesome when we lack a stable identity of our own, so we begin taking on *too much* of the people around us. This phenomenon is most notably observed in patients with personality disorders, where they mimic not just small social cues — but big things too — like your hopes, dreams, hobbies, and insecurities.

When someone copies your entire personality, it's not a sign of empathy.

It's a sign of the complete opposite.

Solitary sucks, but I'm an introvert. I've gone a lot longer than twenty-four hours without human interaction, so I knew I'd be able to survive this.

Still, after four hours alone with my thoughts, I'll admit I felt a wave of relief when I heard that first whisper.

"*Hello?*"

I raised my eyebrows and examined the air vent by my side.

"*Hi,*" I whispered back. "What's your name?"

"Elliot," the voice responded.

"Oh," I said with a laugh. "That's my name too."

"What are the odds?" he laughed too. "Are you also in here for pissing off a deranged psychiatrist?"

I felt a strange knot form in the pit of my stomach.

"Very funny…" I said. "How did you know that?"

There was a pause from the other side. "What do you mean?"

"That's *actually* why I'm in here," I said. "Did you really have a run-in with Zhang too?"

"Yes!" said the voice, a bit louder. "She's withholding life-saving medications from me. Does that count as a run-in?"

The knot in my stomach tightened.

"Alright," I said. "Enough of this."

"What are you talking about?" he asked.

"Clearly someone told you why I'm here, and you're just copying my story."

The voice on the other end went quiet for a moment. Then he said, "Is your name Dr. Elliot Harper?"

"Yes," I said. "Are you also claiming to be him?"

"I *am* him," said the voice.

I shook my head. What the hell was going on?

"Okay…" I said. "If you're Dr. Harper, why don't you tell me your deepest childhood secret?"

"Seriously?" he said. "Why would I tell you that?"

I laughed. "Yeah, that's what I figured. You're full of shit."

There was another moment of silence, and then he spoke again.

"I used to burn myself, because I was ashamed of my sexuality."

A wave of dread coursed through my body.

"Okay, what the fuck?" I said, leaning closer to the vent. "Who the hell are you? Did Zhang put you up to this?"

"What are you talking about?" he said. "I'm Dr. Harper."

I bit my lip and inched away from the vent, as if my personality was leaking through it.

Hours passed without any word from the identity thief.

I enjoyed the silence, but something was still nagging in the back of my mind. How did he learn about my history of self-harm? It only came up once, during the trial, and those documents were sealed. There was no way any inmate here had access to them.

"*Hey,*" I whispered into the vent.

A few seconds later, the voice whispered back. "What do you want?"

"I'm having a dilemma," I said. "I have valuable information that Zhang wants. And unless I give it to her soon, I'll most likely end up contracting HIV. You seem to be in the same predicament. So... What do you think we should do?"

My guess was that this imposter was some plant from Zhang to convince me to give up the photo. Hopefully he'd take the bait, and then I could manipulate him into giving me information about Zhang.

I heard a sigh from the other end. "Okay, I'll play along. But only because I'm bored."

Jesus, he even *spoke* like me.

"Great," I said. "So what are you going to do?"

"I'm not going to give up the photo," he said simply. "People live perfectly happy lives with HIV."

That wasn't what I expected. My imposter seemed to have more of a spine than me. And he definitely wasn't trying to convince me to give up the photo.

Not yet, at least.

"If you're really Elliot Harper, you'd understand that this is a spiritual battle," I pressed.

"How so?" he asked.

"My whole life, I've been given this choice between justice and peace," I said. "And every time, I go with justice."

"How has that worked out for you?" he asked. "We're sitting in solitary confinement, with a life sentence."

Bingo.

I pretended to play along with his concerns.

"Exactly," I said. "Justice never works out for me. I'm always trying to control the outcome, because I don't think people can be trusted to do the right thing."

There was a pause from the other end. "So what would happen if you chose peace instead?"

"I don't know, because I've never done it." I laughed. "It's like I keep getting the same test over and over again. And I keep failing it."

"Story of my life," he said.

"The alternative would require more faith, right?"

"What do you mean?" he asked.

"Well," I began, "When I do these self-destructive things for justice, it means I don't have faith in God, right?"

"How do you figure?"

"I'm playing judge and jury, because I don't trust that God will deliver justice," I said. "Which also means I don't accept the gifts being offered to me along the way."

"Gifts?" he said.

"Noah," I said quietly. "My first chance at love, and I threw it away for justice — justice that never even occurred. Now I have this choice between pursuing vigilante justice *yet again*, or saving myself from a life-threatening illness. How much more blatant can these lessons get? How many times do I need this choice from God, before I learn my lesson?"

"You think we're all here to learn a lesson?"

"Yes," I said. "And until we resolve that lesson, it will continue to cause us suffering — in this life, and the next."

We both went quiet for a few minutes.

Hopefully that would be enough for him to believe that he was changing my mind. I couldn't wait to see the look on Dr. Zhang's face when I spat in it.

For the next several hours, we continued talking about spirituality.

It's a bizarre thing, discussing deep personal issues with someone claiming to be you. But it certainly passes the time.

"Hmmm…"

Predictably, Dr. Zhang knocked on the solitary door with only several hours left to take PEP, before it lost all effectiveness. At this point, it was a gamble if it would even work anymore.

"Mr. Harper, I just wanted to give you one final opportunity…" she said. "Have you made your choice?"

"Yes."

My imposter and I answered at the exact same exact time.

"My choice is that you rot in hell," I said. "And you can tell your little pet to back the fuck off."

There was a moment of silence, and then the voice from the next cell spoke.

"The photo is in the showers," he said. "There's a loose tile on the far wall."

My heart screamed. *What the fuck.* How could he possibly know that?

"NO!" I pounded on the door. "NO! HE'S LYING!"

I continued slamming and shouting, but I knew Dr. Zhang was already on her way to the showers.

"How did you know about the tile?" I hissed through the vent.

There was no answer.

"Hey," I said. "How the *fuck* did you know? Are you stalking me in the showers or something?"

Again, I was met only with silence.

Heart racing, I paced around the room, unable to shake the anxiety surging through my body.

Dr. Zhang returned several minutes later.

"Thank you for your honesty," she said. "I'm glad we can finally put this matter to rest. Now, let's get you back to your cell so you can start a PEP regimen."

"Wait a minute," I said. "That's not fair! I should be the one getting PEP."

I wasn't about to lose the photo *and* the PEP.

"What?" The other voice spoke up. "I told her where to get the photo!"

"You don't even need PEP!" I said, exasperated. "This was Zhang's deal with *me*. Not—"

"Gentlemen, please..." Dr. Zhang spoke calmly. "As promised, I will provide the prescription to Mr. Harper."

I let out a heavy sigh of relief as the doors to my cell opened.

"HEY!" The imposter screamed. "I GAVE YOU WHAT YOU WANTED!"

I walked out of the cell with Dr. Zhang and she handed me the two orange bottles.

"Thanks," I muttered, unscrewing the caps and swallowing both pills as we walked away.

In the distance, I heard the imposter continue to shout.

"WHAT THE FUCK DO YOU WANT FROM ME? I CHOSE PEACE OVER JUSTICE. I LEARNED MY FUCKING LESSON!"

Jesus Christ... What a lunatic.

Later that night, I finished writing out the patient file and set my pencil aside — ready to finally get some sleep after this whole fiasco.

I surveyed the mess around me. Pieces of paper strewn about the floor. Hundreds of documents, court transcripts, and news articles. Videotapes and photographs from the trial.

Those were all very helpful in absorbing his personality, but in the end, it was one single essay that gave me a window into his soul:

The intersection of psychology and spirituality, by Dr. Elliot Harper Psy.D.

Dated six years ago, it painted the picture of a deeply rational man with one glaring exception: his relationship with God.

He did not believe in demons, ghosts, or anything remotely paranormal. Yet, he took solace in the idea that we humans are all connected by an "energy" that surges through everything in this universe.

When it came to psychology, he believed that most suffering could be traced back to old emotional wounding — trauma that blocked the connected energy from flowing freely through our bodies, causing us to instead feel isolated, fearful, and defective.

Dr. Harper believed that we were here on Earth to resolve those wounds, and re-connect with the universe around us.

All I had to do was remind him of his own beliefs.

He longed for hope and reason amongst all the chaos. He was comforted by the idea of a divine plan. And so, when I presented the plan to him, he did the rest of the work for me. He assumed I was the voice of God, or at the very least, a blatant sign from God to learn his lesson.

I tossed his essay in the trash, along with the rest of the documents. As tempting as it was to hang onto his identity, I knew it was time to recalibrate.

Recalibration is my least favorite part of this process.

When I take on someone else's identity, my mind is filled with their hopes, dreams, hobbies, and insecurities. I think like them. I talk like them. I *become* them.

But when I shed it all away, I am left only with a crippling sensation of emptiness.

Maybe that's the type of wound Dr. Harper was referring to in his essay.

Maybe he could help me.

But Dr. Zhang helps me in a different way. She teaches me how to fill the emptiness by taking on identities and personas from other people. She gives me materials so that I can study everything about them.

The problem is, the relief doesn't last long.

A single identity is never enough to fill the void. It's like an addiction that gets duller with continued tolerance. Eventually the emptiness comes creeping back. So I have to recalibrate, to prepare for a new identity.

I stripped off all of my clothes, and I began saying goodbye to Dr. Harper's personality — irritable, judgmental, and a bit paranoid. He was an unpleasant man, but for some reason, I very much enjoyed being him.

I reached over to the desk and pumped eight squirts of BioFreeze onto my palms.

BioFreeze is a menthol-based gel that creates an intense cold-burning sensation on the skin. It is meant for spot treatment on a sore back or shoulder, but I rub it all over my entire body.

It's very important to cover every inch of the body — including eyelids, scalp, lips, anus, and genitals. This completes the seal.

Within minutes, the freezing heat kicks in.

My body is on fire. And yet, I am rolling in a fresh coat of snow on Christmas morning.

I lay on the floor and I make snow angels as I feel Dr. Harper exiting my body.

Tears stream down my face. The loss is painful, and it leaves me with a profound sense of loneliness.

The snow is grey. The sky is grey. Everything is grey.

Everything is empty.

Dr. Harper tries to come back in, but he cannot. The burning ice shield protects me.

The shield protects my body from all of the previous visitors.

Nobody can come back inside.

Especially not the screaming children.

End of Patient File: The Copy Cat

Dr. Harper Therapy Company Retreat

The Copy Cat

"What's taking the police so long to get here?"

I paced around anxiously as James rested.

"I don't know," said Noah. "Should I call again?"

I sighed and shook my head. "No. It's just — something is really wrong here."

"What do you mean?" he asked.

I lowered my voice. "His stories... It's like he's been — I don't know — kidnapped or something."

Noah raised his eyebrows. "You really think it's that serious?"

"Think about what he's told us!" I whispered. "Someone recruiting little kids. Another person drugging them..."

"Could he just have an active imagination?" suggested Noah.

"He's too young to be talking about things like that," I said. "And what if the police don't understand or believe his story?"

"Well, maybe you can keep seeing him as a patient," he said. "You're so good at figuring people out."

"At this point, you're doing a better job of therapist

than me."

"Then we could help him together," said Noah. "I've always wanted to try that!"

He looked into my eyes, like he wanted to say something more. But before we could continue, James began shouting.

"SHUT UP. SHUT UP. SHUT UP."

We both hurried over to him.

"What's wrong?" asked Noah.

"I hate him!" said James. "He pretends to be me, but he's not!"

"Who?" I pressed.

"The copy cat."

"Another animal?" said Noah. "Don't worry, we can make him go away."

"You can't," said James. "Even when he's gone, his whispers stay in my head."

Noah looked at me, unsure of what to say next.

"What does he whisper to you?" I asked.

"He says that he is me — he is James. He says that I like the bad thing. He says that I ask for it."

"What is the bad thing?"

James gave me a miserable look, so I did not push the subject.

"I'm sorry," I said, changing the topic. "Can you tell me more about how he copies you?"

James sniffled. "He knows everything about me. He knows my favorite color. He knows the names of my stuffed animals. He knows about the time my sister fell off the swings — and he knows how it made me feel scared."

Noah and I glanced at each other, at a loss for words.

"He copies my voice too," said James. "He laughs like me. And when I cry, he cries too."

"Well, he's *not* you," I said firmly. "You're the *only* you, okay? In fact, he's your opposite!"

James looked at me. "My opposite?"

"Yes," I said. "I bet he didn't look like you, did he?"

James shook his head. "No. He was tall and minty."

I frowned. "Minty?"

"Yes," said James. "He always smelled minty. Like a cough drop."

Cannibal Conscience

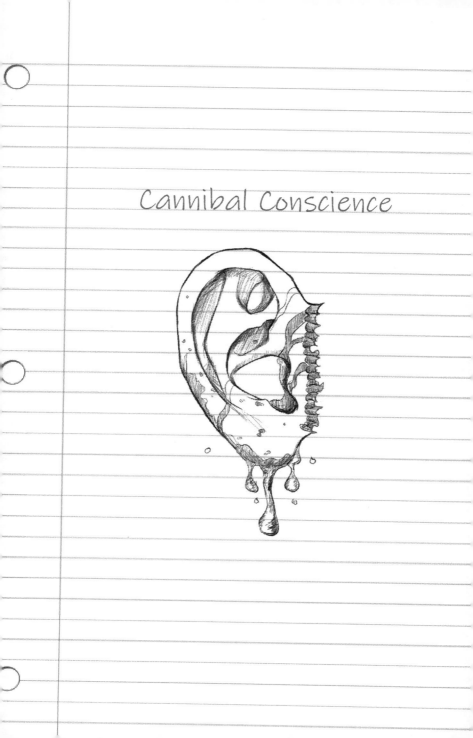

Cannibal Conscience

PART ONE

Though psychopaths make up roughly 1% of the general male adult population, they make up between 15% and 25% of the males incarcerated in North American prison systems. There is no other variable that is more highly correlated to being in prison than psychopathy.

- Kent A. Kiehl, Ph.D. ; Jurimetrics: The Journal of Law, Science, and Technology

"Yo, are psychopaths born or made?"

The infamous cannibal known as *'The Zombie'* sat across from me at my usual lunch spot.

But he didn't look like a serial killer at all. He looked like a college jock — like one of those guys at the gym who constantly lifts up their shirt to look at their own abs in the mirror.

"It really depends, Chase," I said. "For a lot of people, it can be combination of both."

"Nah, not for me, Doctor H."

He sounded like a college jock too.

"Which do you align with?"

"Gotta be nature," he said. "I know you're a therapist and all, so gotta ask about my childhood, but my childhood was freakin' awesome."

"Well—"

"And I know you're gonna talk about repressed memories and shit, but that's not what happened either."

"It could have happened long before you were even aware," I said. "People think infants are blobs of flesh with no emotional memory, but the body can hold onto wounding — like the sensation of being unwanted by a parent."

He stared at me blankly for several seconds, clearly bored, and then changed the subject. "Yo, Doctor H, should I tell you how I killed people? Will that help you fix me?"

I swallowed, but tried to appear calm. "Okay."

"I hung out on the streets, dressed as a homeless dude," he said. "I sat in a wheelchair, and I added wrinkles and dirt with makeup — so I looked like a grandpa."

"Why?"

He shrugged. "People who give money to bums are more trusting... caring... gullible."

"So you preyed on the kindness of others. Got it."

"Yo, don't get judgy with *me*!" said Chase defensively. "I wasn't the one picking them."

I frowned. "What do you mean?"

He leaned across the table and began flexing his left bicep for no reason.

"*I'm not guilty*," he whispered seriously, like it was some huge revelation. "I forget the word for it... What's it called when one of those huge-ass trucks loses control and accidentally rams another car, killing the driver?"

"In most cases, that would be considered manslaughter."

"Yeah, that's it!" he exclaimed, continuing to admire his bicep. "At worst, I'm a manslaughter — er."

"This wasn't accidental!" I said incredulously. "You murdered and ate people."

"Yo, I didn't have any *control*!" He slammed his fists on the table. "Didn't you see the videos, Doctor H? I always punched myself after. But when I'm told to kill in the moment, I *have* to kill."

"How can you *have* to do anything?" I said. "Especially kill?"

"Alright..." He sighed, as if it should have been obvious.

86

"Lemme explain it for you. Think about something you feel like you *gotta* do — you a smoker?"

"No."

"Booze, then."

"I don't drink."

He glared at me in annoyance. "Jerking off."

I felt my cheeks go red.

"Finally," he muttered. "So think about how it feels when you've gone a week without... that."

"That's completely different—"

"Then multiply that feeling by a thousand," he said. "*That's* what I feel in the moment when I'm told to eat."

"Who the hell is telling you to *eat someone*?" I snapped.

He started making a duck face, like he was posing for a photo, even though no one was taking a picture.

"Coach Adam."

I raised my eyebrows. "Coach?"

"Yeah, I was on the football team," he said. "Quarterback."

"And your *coach* was telling you to eat people?"

"Yeah," he said. "During bulking season — for the protein."

I stared at him in disbelief.

"So your coach... Was telling you to consume other humans... For protein."

"Exactly!" He let out a sigh of relief and sprawled back in his chair. "I knew you'd believe me, Doctor H."

"What?" I sputtered. "I don't believe you!"

But he wasn't listening to me anymore. Instead, he was leaning back in his chair and throwing an imaginary football through the air.

Chase had to be the most vain, self-absorbed patient I'd ever met — admiring his muscles while casually talking about murdering people. I definitely agreed with whichever court-ordered psychiatrist diagnosed him as a narcissistic sociopath, but I still wanted to learn why he came to talk with me today.

So I decided to play along.

"Chase, does Coach Adam still tell you to hurt people in prison?"

"Nah." He shook his head. "Haven't seen him since I got here."

"So... Without him around, do you still feel compelled to kill?"

"Nope," he said, sitting back up in his chair. "Well, not until last week. That's why I need your help."

"What happened last week?"

Chase made another duck face and began stroking his bicep affectionately.

"Got a new coach."

I leaned forward. "Someone else is telling you to kill?"

I was 99% sure that he was projecting his own murderous urges onto these imaginary "coaches" to deflect the blame from himself, but I still wanted to hear his entire story before I jumped to any conclusions.

"That's why I came to you, Doctor H," he said. "I need you to build me a conscience — otherwise I think I'm gonna do something really bad."

I raised my eyebrows. "Worse than killing and eating people...?"

For the first time in our conversation, he actually looked uncomfortable.

"I don't wanna talk about it," he mumbled, toying with his food.

"Wait a minute..." I said. "Chase, what exactly does this new coach want you to do?"

He lifted a chicken wing from his lunch tray and tossed the entire thing into his mouth — bones and all.

"Just build me a conscience, okay?"

As he chewed, I couldn't help but notice the horrible crunching sound.

PART TWO

I spent my rec hour scanning through newspapers in the library, looking for headlines about Chase.

We're not allowed to use Google in prison, but fortunately stories about *The Zombie* have dominated most major papers for the past year.

Flipping through months of records, I also came across several articles about my own trial:

Doctor of Horror: The Psychiatrist Who Stalked and Tortured his Patients

Elliot Harper Receives Life Sentence for Kidnapping Cop Family

Is Therapy Safe? 10 Simple Tips to Avoid 'Professionals' like Dr. Harper

I closed my eyes and took a deep breath. A familiar sensation of embarrassment was stirring somewhere deep within my stomach.

I turned back to the papers and continued going back in time, until I finally started seeing stories about *The Zombie*.

Zombie Killer on Trial for Cannibalizing Seven Victims

College Student Slammed with Eight Life Sentences for 'Zombie' Murders

Chase Collins: Did Hazing Rituals Cause Star Quarterback to Snap?

The last one caught my eye, so I pulled out the newspaper and began reading the article:

Throughout the highly publicized trial, dozens of witnesses took the stand to testify against Chase Collins.

But one person came forward to defend him.

Speaking under the condition of anonymity, a classmate described a series of hazing rituals in the months leading up to Collins' murder spree.

However, Collins himself denied these rumors and shouted at the witness: "Shut up, f*ggot!"

The football team's coach, Adam Driscoll, also denied any wrongdoing. "The university has a strict policy against hazing and initiation rituals. Chase was a promising young quarterback, and he was welcomed onto the team with open arms." (Continued on Page 3B).

I flipped to 3B, curious to learn more about Driscoll — or "Coach Adam", as Chase called him. But the rest of the article was just filled with speculation and professional opinions about the psychological impact of hazing.

I turned back to the front page to check for the article's author — perhaps they had written more on the topic. But when I saw the name, I raised my eyebrows.

"No way…"

"Elliot!"

My heart lurched with the same anxiety I felt every time I saw Zach.

"Hi," I said awkwardly as he pulled me into a close hug.

Our friendship was a simple one: I had a childhood crush on him, he informed me that he was straight, so we decided to become friends who had tea together every month.

Except now — instead of tea — we met in the prison's visitor center.

"Alright, break it off." The guard pushed us apart, and then chuckled to himself. "Heh. Strange seeing a black man visit a white man in prison, right?"

I screwed up my face and opened my mouth to tell him off, but Zach touched my shoulder and motioned for me to sit down.

I sighed and sank into the chair. Zach sat across from me and gave me an encouraging smile, which only made me feel more self-conscious about the fact that I was a prisoner, and he was not.

"Listen, I need you to look something up for me."

Zach laughed. "It's nice to see you too, Elliot."

"Sorry," I said quickly. "It's just, this is important. It's for a patient."

He gave me an odd look. "You're seeing patients in here?"

"Well — sort of," I said. "It's complicated."

"Okay..." he said hesitantly. "What do you need?"

"Adam Driscoll," I said. "The Zombie's football coach. You mentioned him in an article. I need to know everything about him. Anything you can find."

Zach's eyes went wide. "Elliot, please tell me you're not trying to treat a serial killer..."

"Will you just trust me?" I said. "You know I wouldn't ask unless it was important."

He gave me a forced smile and nodded. "I'll see what I can find."

Zach was an investigative journalist with a major newspaper, so he had access and police contacts that could hopefully help him figure this out. Which reminded me—

"Hey," I lowered my voice. "Any news on Noah?"

Zach's face flooded with guilt, which meant I already had my answer.

"Elliot, I've been looking, I promise," he said. "I still haven't found anything."

It was the same answer he'd given me since the day I got here. No updates, no leads, nothing about my missing assistant. If it was anyone but Zach, I might have guessed that he wasn't even looking at all.

But this was Zach, and I knew I could trust him with my life.

"Alright," I said. "Well, just check out this Driscoll guy, okay? I really think it could help with this patient."

Zach nodded reluctantly and then let out a sigh.

"Elliot..." he began. "I just have to ask, are you being safe in here?"

I frowned. "What do you mean?"

"There are rumors..." he said nervously. "I have connections in the prison... And I heard that you..."

"What have you heard?" I demanded.

He looked down and fidgeted with his fingers.

"Zach, tell me."

He cleared his throat. "I heard — I heard you may have… gotten HIV."

"Jesus," I muttered as my anxiety worsened.

"Is it true?" he asked.

"Yes, probably," I said. "But it's a long story—"

"They also said you were caught with a young inmate. Is that — is that how it happened?"

"For fuck's sake, Zach!" I stood up. "Are you going to believe everything you hear from your *connections*? We've been friends for two decades."

His eyes shifted to the left and he lowered his voice. "I'm just saying, I worried about you."

I shook my head and brushed past him.

"I expect this bullshit from everyone else, but not from you."

"Elliot—"

"No!" I spun around. "Do you have any idea how humiliating it is to stand here in this orange jumpsuit, while you sit there judging me? And now you think I'm some sort of sexual predator—"

"I'm sorry!" He stood up too. "I made a mistake, okay? Truce?"

He stuck out his hand.

I stared at it for a moment, but did not shake it.

"Adam Driscoll," I said flatly, turning to leave. "Figure it out."

As I walked away from the table, I heard him mutter: "*Pleasant as ever, Elliot…*"

I stuck up my middle finger and stormed away.

The following day in the prison yard, I sat on the bleachers while Chase did pushups by my feet.

"Can you tell me more about the football team?" I asked.

"What do you wanna know?"

"Were you close with them?"

He switched to one arm and looked up at me. "Yeah, we were tight. Why?"

"Well, I heard a witness talked about hazing."

Chase scoffed and shook his head.

"Was there any truth to it?" I asked. "I mean, you were a freshman recruit. Hazing is almost expected."

"No," he said. "Okay? Nobody hazed me."

After a moment of consideration, I decided to persist. "Then why do you think the witness said it happened?"

Chase switched to planks.

"Jenkins was a faggot who wanted to fuck half the team," he said. "Probably wanted to get in my pants."

I didn't flinch. "Chase, therapy only works if you're honest with me."

"Yo, I *am* being honest!" he said, dropping to the ground. "Why are you being a dick about it?"

"You asked me to build you a conscience," I said. "I can't do that if you're lying. What kind of hazing was it? Drinking? Physical?... *Sexual?*"

His face went dark red.

"Fuck off, Doctor H."

"Chase, there's no shame in—"

"I said fuck off." He stood up. "Leave me alone."

"Hazing can leave long-lasting damage—"

He lunged forward and punched me in the face.

"FUCK OFF, FAGGOT!"

As he walked away, I touched my face and felt blood pouring from my nose.

I probably deserved that.

―――――――― // ――――――――

I lay on my bed later in the evening and changed out the tissues in my nose.

I knew it was wrong to push Chase on a topic that clearly made him uncomfortable, but if he actually had a healthy childhood (as he claimed), this alleged hazing incident was the only clue to his sudden shift in behavior.

"Harper."

I jumped at the sound of someone at our cell door.

Hopping off the bed, I looked through the bars and saw the same guard from the visitor center. Pickowitz, I think was his name.

"Yeah?"

He handed me a small brown paper bag. "This is for you."

I frowned and accepted the package.

"And if you need anything in here, just let me know, okay?"

"Uh — okay..."

He gave me a thumbs up and walked away.

"Wow, VIP status..." Tony sat up from his bed. "Who paid off Pickowitz for you?"

"I have no idea," I said, bringing the bag up to my bed.

I opened it and sprinkled a few items onto my sheets.

First was an OraQuick box — the HIV home test kit. Next was a Ziplock bag of pills. Upon further inspection, I quickly identified them as Truvada.

And finally, a note.

I unfolded it and immediately recognized Zach's handwriting.

Elliot,

I know you're pissed at me, but please just take the test and — if positive — use the pills to keep your viral load down.

If you need anything in there, Pickowitz will help you out.

I looked into Adam Driscoll. His file is locked, but I did some digging and found his ID linked to some heavily redacted government projects. I don't know what you've gotten yourself into, but please stay far away from this.

Driscoll works for the CIA.

PART THREE

"Chase, I'm sorry about yesterday."

"Leave me alone," he mumbled, sliding his tray down the lunch table.

I followed and sat down across from him.

"Listen, I don't think you were hazed," I said quickly. "And I think I can build you a conscience."

His eyes lit up. "Yo, really?"

"Well, sort of," I said. "I think you actually already have one. It's just been buried deep down."

He nodded seriously. "I bet that's why I punch myself after eating people!"

"Exactly," I said. "That's the part of you that feels shame, remorse, and guilt. But you're disconnected from it."

He made a duck face. "Like a shoulder."

"No... Not like a shoulder." I stared at him. "Think of your body and emotions like a highway."

"Body's a highway. Got it."

"Now, imagine there's a huge crash — 20 car pileup — so the police block off the highway and re-route traffic off an earlier exit. The detour works, but it uses more gas and takes you through a shady part of town. Months later, the cops *still* won't let you back on the highway. Don't you want to know why?"

"Yeah, what's taking them so long?"

"They can't clean it up," I said. "So they're hoping you'll keep taking the detour forever."

"That's bullshit!" He smacked the table. "I want to get back on the highway."

"Chase, the thing you have to understand is that our bodies and minds don't create a 'detour' unless we've experienced some pretty serious trauma. If we want to get back on the highway, we have to be ready to see the crash."

He crossed his arms. "I can handle it."

"Great," I said. "I'd like to try an alternative therapy with you. It's called Somatic Experiencing. It focuses on body sensations that arise from trauma, and I think it can help you get back on the highway."

"That's bomb."

"Yeah, it's pretty cool," I said. "Now, since I don't really have an office, are you comfortable doing it here?"

He shrugged. "Whatever."

"Okay," I said. "We're going to experiment with entering the disregulated state."

"The what?"

"The crash on the highway," I corrected myself. "So in order to get there, I need to know what triggers the murders. How exactly did Coach Adam tell you to kill your victims?"

Chase looked down.

"It's okay," I said. "You can take your time."

After a few moments, Chase mumbled: "Bulk up, skinny faggot."

"Chase, come on. I'm trying to help you."

"No, that's what he says to me!" said Chase. "He points to the person I'm supposed to kill, and says *bulk up, skinny faggot.* Just don't ever say those words around me, okay?"

"Understood." I raised my eyebrows. "And how does it feel when he says it to you?"

He rolled his eyes. "It feels *great,* Doctor H."

"Sorry, dumb question," I said. "Can you describe any body sensations that come up when you think of that phrase?"

"I dunno," he mumbled. "I'm not gonna start crying like some pussy, if that's what you're after."

"Focus, Chase," I said. "Close your eyes and do a body scan from the top down… Start with your head. How does it feel?"

He closed his eyes and shook his head. "It feels like a fucking head."

"Now your neck," I said.

"I don't know," he said. "Like a neck? Or a throat?"

"Good," I said. "Heart?"

"Fuck, Doctor H!" He opened his eyes. "You're annoying as fuck, anyone ever told you that?"

"Yes, actually." I nodded. "Now, please close your eyes and focus on your heart. Any unusual sensations?"

He sighed and closed his eyes again. After a few seconds, he shook his head.

"And now your stomach," I said. "Anything there?"

He touched his stomach. "Hungry as usual."

"Good," I said. "Can you tell me more about this hunger feeling?"

"What, you never been hungry before?"

"I'd like to hear you describe it."

He shook his head. "It feels — I dunno. Empty."

There we go.

"Can you describe what emptiness feels like?" I asked.

He looked visibly irritated with my questions, but answered: "Like a... black hole. No matter how much I put in, it's never enough."

"There's your highway crash," I said with a smile. "You can open your eyes."

He frowned. "I have a car crash in my stomach?"

"Yes, I'd guess that's where the pain lives," I said. "Do you want to go further?"

"Fuck yeah," he said, lifting up his shirt and rubbing his abs. "Yoooo! Hello in there!"

Talking to the physical sensation actually wasn't a bad idea... But a crowded lunch room was possibly the worst place to dive deeper into trauma. Then I remembered the guard — Pickowitz — had offered to help me.

"Chase," I said, standing up. "I'm going to see if I can get us some privacy for the next part."

"Why?" He made a duck face. "You wanna get in my pants?"

"Will you fucking stop with that?" I snapped. "Just because I'm gay doesn't mean I'm attracted to you. Do you want to bang every woman you meet?"

"Well, only the hot ones—"

"Exactly. And I don't think you're hot. At all."

He frowned and looked genuinely offended. "Then what do you want privacy for?"

"Because we're going to explore what caused the highway crash," I said. "When everything went empty."

"I journaled through it all," he said. "You think that would help?"

I stared at him incredulously. "You're just telling me this now?"

"So it would help?"

"*Yes, Chase...*" I sighed and rubbed my eyes. "It would help."

That night, I sat in bed and read through hundreds of pages from Chase's notebook.

Earlier entries painted the picture of a pretty typical college freshman — enthusiastic, slightly insecure, and eager to find a sense of belonging.

He met his girlfriend, Sara, through a 10am Intro to Sociology class.

He partied and drank like everyone else in college, but nothing out of the ordinary.

He joined the football team, and was quickly welcomed thanks to his skills on the field.

He built a strong bond with the football coach, who he described as a "second dad".

Basically, he seemed like a promising young athlete who was on track to enjoy the ideal college experience.

But some time around his second semester, everything started to change.

April 21
Dinner at Coach Adam's tonight. Whole team is gonna be there!

April 22
Blacked out last night. No idea what happened. I didn't even drink that much.

April 24
Guys on the team are acting weird around me. Hope they get over it for playoffs next week.

April 27
Bombed final exams. Thought I did pretty well, but failed every single one. Going to lose my scholarship.

April 29
What the fuck is happening to my life. The guys are calling me a fag and sending around some picture. No one will show it to me.

April 30
Just kill me. During playoffs, people passed around a picture of me with some guy. Whole crowd was laughing. I swear I never did the shit in that picture.

May 1

Sara dumped me. I hate my fucking life. Everywhere I go on campus, people just laugh at me. Feels like I'm going insane. My mind won't stop racing. My body hurts.

May 3

Someone sent the picture to my dad. He told me not to come home this summer. I seriously think I might be suicidal.

May 5

Coach Adam said I can stay with him. He's the only person who's still good to me.

May 14

Moved in with Coach Adam. He says he'll try to get me back on the football team, but I've gotta bulk up. At this point I'll do anything he says. I just want my life back.

June 19

I've started having blackouts. I think I might be doing some really bad shit. Coach Adam says it's time to stop journaling for a while.

The next day, Chase and I sat outside on an unusually chilly summer day.

"Chase, have you ever heard of Ted Kaczynski?"

"Who's that?" he asked.

"The Unabomber," I said. "He killed multiple people in the 80s with mail bombs."

"Never heard of him." He shrugged. "Why's he important?"

I took a deep breath before continuing with my very far-fetched hypothesis.

"Before his murder spree, Kaczynski was the subject of a government experiment."

He leaned forward excitedly. "Yo, like aliens and shit?"

"No," I said. "A psychological experiment."

He looked disappointed. "Oh."

"It was actually quite serious," I said. "A professor befriended him, and he was asked to share his most personal beliefs about morals, humans, and philosophy."

Chase yawned. "You're losing me, Doctor H."

"Kaczynski trusted this professor, and formed a strong bond with him. The professor's validation meant a great deal to him — almost like a parent."

Chase snorted.

"But the experiment was all about stress and humiliation," I continued. "So the professor eventually began tearing apart Kaczynski's deepest beliefs and personality traits. Fellow peers and instructors relentlessly mocked him — taunting and screaming at him until he was reduced to tears and panic attacks."

"That's fucked up," Chase mumbled. "But what does that have to do with the bomb shit?"

"Chase, it's extremely painful to experience betrayal and abuse from the people we trust most," I said. "Humans are social beings — we thrive on a sense of approval and belonging. But when we experience disgust and exile from others, that's when the agonizing sensation of shame is born."

He swallowed. "The highway crash?"

"Yes, exactly!" I exclaimed. "I think Coach Adam *intentionally created* that crash inside of you."

"What the fuck? Why?"

"Because when you reduce someone to toxic shame, you destroy their core identity. Then you can create the detour around the crash, and design it in a way that suits you. It's a form of mind control."

"Why would he want to control my mind?"

"A friend of mine found links between Coach Adam and the CIA," I said. "I think he was trying to groom you as a weapon — an asset. First, he gave you the world: popularity, success, and belonging. Then he manufactured public shame and humiliation, pushing away your entire support network. And finally, he stepped in as your savior. The process is actually a lot like an abusive relationship."

"You think he made up that picture?"

I paused for a moment. "I think he drugged you and photographed you in a precarious situation. And then I think he distributed the picture at the game — and sent it to your father."

Chase kicked a pebble on the ground.

"And when he tells you to bulk up—"

"Don't!" said Chase.

"Sorry," I said quickly. "When he gives you... the command to kill, I think it activates the old wounding and humiliation. It messes up all of your brain chemicals and gives you this overwhelming compulsion to resolve the shame by doing whatever the savior says."

"So how do I *stop* it!" Chase slammed his fists onto the bleachers. "I have to learn how to *stop* myself, before the new coach tells me to..."

He cleared his throat and looked down.

"Chase," I leaned forward seriously. "I need you to tell me who your new coach is, and what they want you to do."

He shook his head.

"Chase," I repeated his name. "I know your killing command, and I would never use it against you. You can trust me. But this other person... They're using you. Just like Coach Adam."

"Yo, how the fuck do I know I can trust *you*, Doctor H? What if this is just another experiment!"

"Because, I would never use a psychological condition against you," I said gently. "I'm trying to help you *fight* it."

Before I could get another word out of him, we were interrupted by Pickowitz.

"Harper. Collins. Come with me." Then he laughed. "Heh. Isn't that a book or something?"

"It's a publishing house," I said.

"Well, come with me," said Pickowitz. "Dr. Zhang wants to see you."

I frowned. "Both of us?"

"Yep. Both of you."

At this point, the mere act of sitting in Dr. Zhang's office gave me anxiety.

Chase and I sat on the couch across from her desk, waiting for her to say something. For at least a minute, all she did was gaze at us and smile.

But I had learned my lesson. I would never be the first to speak in her office.

"Mr. Collins," she finally began. "The guards tell me that you've been spending a lot of time with Mr. Harper these days."

He nervously began inspecting his bicep. "Yeah, and what's it to you?"

"Well, it's just that Mr. Harper has a worrisome reputation of trying to psychologically 'treat' inmates here," she said. "And thus far, all of his 'patients' have ended up dead or seriously wounded."

I bit my tongue, trying to remain silent.

"I'm just trying to keep you safe," said Dr. Zhang with a smile. "You're my patient, and I care very much for you."

"Y—You do?" he asked.

"That's right." She nodded. "So I need you to tell me why you're spending time with Mr. Harper. You haven't been telling him about our little sessions, have you?"

My eyes went wide.

Jesus Christ, was Zhang the new 'coach' he'd been talking about?

"Chase, she's manipulating you," I said quickly, ignoring my better instinct to keep quiet. "I can help you, but you need to trust me."

"*Hmmm…*" said Dr. Zhang, staring intently at Chase. "Now why on Earth would you trust a dangerous prisoner over a licensed psychiatrist?"

"Because I have nothing to gain from helping you," I answered. "I want to get you back on the highway — so we can fix the crash. But first, you have to tell me what she wants you to—"

"Mr. Collins," Dr. Zhang interrupted me. "I can get you back on the football team. But not if you're listening to liars like Mr. Harper."

Chase's eyes darted back and forth between the two of us, trying to figure out who to trust.

"You can't get back on the football team." I shook my head. "Anyone who promises that is lying to you. But I can help you find something much better."

"What?" he demanded. "What's better than the football team?"

"You can feel peace and happiness in your own body again," I said. "You can feel light and free, instead of that empty black hole in your stomach."

To my surprise, Chase's eyes began to water. It was his first display of true emotion since we'd met.

"Mr. Harper is trying to seduce you. He's a sexual predator—"

"She kidnapped a bunch of kids!" Chase stood up and pointed at Dr. Zhang. "She wants me to eat the ones they kill, so there's no evidence left behind."

What the fuck.

Dr. Zhang's eyes glowered. "Nonsense. That's enough—"

"Yo, it's not nonsense!" he shouted. "You told me I'm

supposed to replace the current guy who disposes kids — you said he's burning their bodies!"

"Who?" I stood up too. "Who's burning the kids?"

"ENOUGH!"

"Chase, tell me who you're replacing!" I pleaded. "Who's hurting these kids?"

Chase nodded anxiously. "You know him. He's—"

"BULK UP, SKINNY FAGGOT!" Dr. Zhang shrieked and pointed at me.

Chase immediately got a frenzied look in his eyes and lunged toward me.

"No!" I gasped. "Remember the crash on the highway!"

He bit into my arm and I felt pain surge through my body.

"Please stop," I pleaded. "You can fight this."

"I can't!" he growled. He bit me again, this time in the stomach. I fell to the ground in agony.

Dr. Zhang stood by her desk, her expression a mix of fascination and excitement as she watched her latest weapon at work.

Laying on the ground, helpless and exposed, I continued begging Chase to stop.

"You're not what they said you are, Chase. You were abused and manipulated."

He pinned me down and knelt over me, locking his mouth around my ear.

"Please, Chase." I squirmed to get away. "Listen to your conscience. Those kids need your help."

Finally he stopped for a moment and ran his tongue along the inside of my ear. He was breathing heavily and grunting — almost like he was fighting against himself.

And then, in a barely audible whisper, he croaked:

"I'm replacing your cellmate, Doctor H."

But before I could even process Chase's words, he moaned with pleasure and bit my ear off.

End of Patient File: The Dragon

Dr. Harper Therapy Company: R—a

The Dragon

"James, the police are almost here," I said gently. "After you're home, would you like to keep talking with us?"

James looked at Noah.

"I'll be there!" said Noah. "We can keep telling stories together."

I was shocked to see James jump up from the ground and run into Noah's arms.

"Will you be my new dad?"

"Oh!" Noah bent down to his level. "Well, I can't be your dad, but I'd love to be your friend! Will you be my friend?"

James nodded. "And you'll keep me safe from the dragon?"

Noah raised his eyebrows. "There's a dragon out there?"

"Yes," said James. "But he only comes when we're in trouble."

I bent down next to them. "What kind of trouble?"

"Sometimes a boy says no. He fights. And that makes them mad."

"So they send a dragon?"

"Uh huh," said James. "After the hornet puts the boy to sleep, and then the dragon comes."

"What does the dragon do?" I asked.

His eyes were glazed over, reflecting only the stormy

ocean behind him.

"He comes in the middle of the night," said James. "He takes the sleeping boy, and lights him on fire."

"Doc!" Noah whispered. "Please stop. We need to wait for the police"

But James continued. "It smells like a barbecue. And then I never see him again."

"I'm so sorry," I said softly. "James, have you ever seen the dragon? Can you tell us what he looks like? Maybe we can help catch him."

"I saw him once," said James. "He was missing teeth."

"Anything else?" I pressed.

James thought for a moment, and then added:

"His arm — it was in a sling."

False Flag

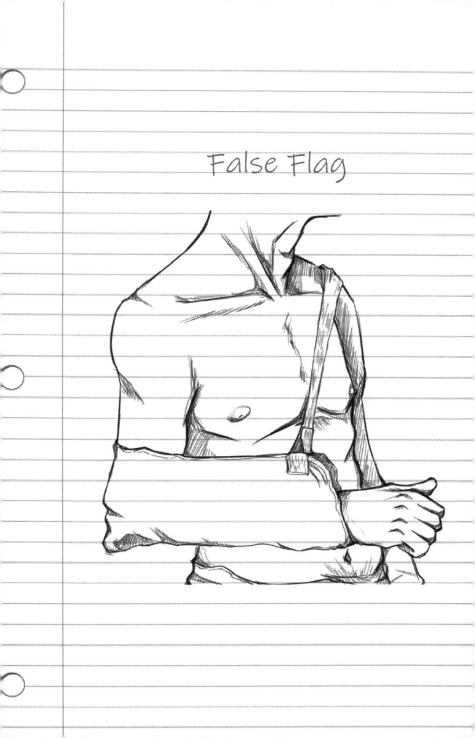

False Flag

PART ONE

"What are you writing?" I asked Tony.

"Letters."

"To who?" I pressed.

He looked up from his bed.

"You know, doc, in all our time together, you've never once taken an interest in my writing. Why the sudden shift?"

I bit my lip. "Just curious."

At this point, neither Tony nor Dr. Zhang knew what Chase had told me, so I was just trying to play dumb while I pried for more details. I couldn't ask Chase, because he had been sent to solitary after attacking me. Thankfully Pickowitz heard my screams and restrained him before I lost any more than my ear.

"Well, if you must know, I'm writing to the supposed 'survivors' of SlapDot."

I frowned. The SlapDot bombing was over two years ago. Sixteen social media employees died that day, and twelve were left with horrific injuries.

"That's nice," I said. "But why are you sending them condolences all this time later?"

"Condolences?" He snorted. "No, doc. These are death threats."

"What?" I hopped down from my bunk and stood next to him, certain that I must have heard him incorrectly through the bandage on my ear. "Did you say *death threats*?"

"Yeah."

I screwed up my face. "Why the hell would you do that?"

"Because the bombing didn't happen," snapped Tony. "The
whole thing was staged. Those 'survivors' are crisis actors. They
just hired a bunch of amputees—"

"*Jesus Christ…*" I muttered. Most of the time, I managed to
have a sense of humor about his ridiculous conspiracies. But this
just pissed me off.

"Tony, you can't send those letters."

He continued writing intently. "Why not?"

"Because, those people have already gone through
unimaginable grief and trauma," I said. "You need to let them
heal in peace."

He laughed. "If the bombing actually happened, I would
agree with you."

"It *did* happen," I insisted. "If anyone's faking injuries, it's
you with that stupid fucking arm sling."

He glared at me. "This protects me from—"

"Mind control chem trails," I finished for him. "You've told
me. Well those people *actually* lost their limbs. For fuck's sake, it
was captured on video."

"Videos can be faked," said Tony, nursing his non-existent
injury. "Evidence is always fabricated in these events."

"What events?"

"False flags," said Tony. "They manufacture these tragedies
to make us afraid. That way they can control us — take away
our weapons, regulate everything, make us complacent."

"Who's *they?*"

He looked up. "What do you mean?"

"You keep referring to this omniscient 'they' — organizing
these scary events to trick and control you. Who are 'they'?"

He rolled his eyes. "I'm not your patient, doc. Never will be."

"Is it the government? Deep state?" I continued. "I'm
genuinely just curious… What organization has the resources
and means to pull off these tricks every other week? And how
do so many actors manage to stay quiet about these massive
coverups?"

He looked up from his letter. "You know what's funny, doc?
I'm used to skeptics mocking me. But I'm a bit surprised by

you."

"I'm not mocking—"

"Since the day you got here, I've covered your ass. Every piece of information I've shared with you has turned out to be true. And yet you still have the arrogance to make fun of me."

I thought for a moment and realized he actually had a fair point. He had been right about Arthur and Sam. He had swiped the photo for me. He had warned me about Bernard. But most of the other stuff he babbled on about was incoherent nonsense. Even a broken clock was right twice a day.

"Tony, look, I'm not trying to belittle you. I just hate the idea of harassing people who have already suffered so much."

"They haven't suffered!" he said bitterly.

"Okay, but are you 100% certain?" I asked. "I know you're probably able to debunk every piece of evidence from the bombing. But for every single thing you debunk, there's someone out there debunking your debunk. And what if they're correct? What if you're harassing people who have already lost everything?"

"I'm *not!*"

"But what if you are!" I exclaimed. "Even if it's just a tiny chance, doesn't that risk outweigh anything you could possibly gain from insulting some unethical actors?"

"There's *not* a tiny chance," said Tony defensively. "SlapDot never fucking happened."

"But how can you actually know that? Unless you were there that day—"

He threw the letter down on his bed. "I *was* there, doc."

I raised my eyebrows. "What?"

"I was a web developer at SlapDot," he said. "And I'm telling you, *nobody fucking died.*"

PART TWO

God, I missed the Internet.

Back in the library, I scanned magazines and newspapers for stories to corroborate Tony's claim that he worked for SlapDot.

I was surprised to find that he was actually telling the truth.

In fact, he had been outspoken about the attack since the day it occurred:

SlapDot Employees Puzzled by Colleague's Bizarre Claims

Hours after the bombing at SlapDot's headquarters, one employee vehemently denied that the event took place.

According to a senior developer, Tony Singer, the entire bombing was staged.

"Crisis actors were brought in weeks ago. They planned this whole thing. We had a bunch of trial runs yesterday."

News anchors cut his interview short, but he continued ranting on his SlapDot profile.

"I've never worked with these people. That woman who says she lost both her legs — never met her in my life."

Singer's claims have spread like wildfire on the Internet, serving as fuel for "false flag" conspiracies that often arise after mass tragedies.

I looked up from the article and shook my head in disbelief.

So Tony was telling the truth about working for SlapDot — but was he telling the truth about what happened that day?

"Tony, I wanted to apologize for last night."

"It's alright, doc." He stood up from his bed and stretched. "I'm used to it. When you become a warrior for the truth, you put a target on your back. Ridicule is a favorite tactic of the skeptics."

"It was wrong of me," I said. "I looked up your story, and you were telling the truth. You've been telling me the truth since the beginning."

He gave me a small nod. "I appreciate that."

I took a deep breath. "So I'm going to be honest with you too."

"About what, doc?"

I closed my eyes. This was probably a huge mistake.

"When Chase attacked me, he told me that you…"

Tony raised his eyebrows. "Yes?"

"He — He told me that you're responsible for disposing children."

Tony gave me a grim look.

"That's correct."

"What?" My heart began to race. "Tony — Why? Why would you ever do that?"

Tony sighed. "Can I sit up there with you?"

"Sure," I said, moving over to make room for him.

Tony grunted as he re-adjusted his arm sling, and then climbed up onto the bed.

"Doc, this wasn't how I wanted you to find out," he said quietly. "But I'm the one who's been sending you those letters."

"That was—" I stopped myself and lowered my voice. "*That was you?*"

Someone had been writing anonymous notes to me since the day I arrived, proclaiming their innocence and trying to form some sort of escape alliance. Had I seriously been communicating with my cellmate this whole time?

"I didn't know if I could trust you," he said. "I didn't know if you were working undercover. So I've been testing the waters — with the notes, and the photo."

"Are you working with Zhang?" I asked.

"No!" he exclaimed. "I'm trying to *stop* her. But I can't do it alone."

"What exactly is she doing?"

"She's running a pedophile ring," he said.

"In *prison*?" I asked incredulously.

"Not exactly," said Tony. "But she takes us on 'field trips' to the facility."

"Us?"

"Prisoners," he said. "She uses prisoners to run the whole operation. You've already met most of them."

"Like who?"

"Arthur — he had direct connections with different kids and dark web forums. He basically helped to recruit them. Then there's Bernard — he drugs the kids with tranquilizers and stimulants, depending on the situation."

My eyes went wide. I'm embarrassed to admit, this was the moment where I finally connected our company retreat with the pedophile ring. Every animal the boy told us about was a prisoner here. Except...

"What about the copy cat?" I asked.

"The what?"

"Sorry," I said. "The guy who mimics and brainwashes kids."

Tony nodded darkly. "Richard Scott. He's in cell block B — for strangling his own toddler to death. Couldn't handle the reality of what he did, so he decided to stop being Richard Scott and borrow identities from other people."

"Jesus..." I muttered. "And you? Why are you involved in all this?"

"I swear to God, I'm helping them," he said. "After Bernard overdoses the rejects, I'm supposed to get rid of the bodies. But I always carry Narcan and Adrenaline with me. If I'm able to wake them up, I let them go."

"Wait a minute," I said. "Do you write on their shirts? Things like '*No police*'?"

"Yes." He nodded. "How did you know that?"

"A year back, my assistant and I found a little boy on the beach."

Tony's eyes lit up. "What did he look like?"

I thought back to that day. "Umm... Blonde hair... Green eyes..."

"James!" said Tony happily, eyes tearing up. "Where is he

now?"

I frowned. "What do you mean?"

"Where did you take him?" Tony leaned in close to me. "Is he somewhere safe?"

"I'm not sure. We called the police—"

"NO!"

I jumped, taken aback by Tony's guttural scream.

"What the hell—"

"WHY DID YOU CALL THE POLICE?" he continued shouting. "I PUT IT ON THE FUCKING SHIRT."

"Tony, I didn't—"

"FUCK!" He punched the wall until his knuckles started to bleed. "FUCK. FUCK. FUCK."

"Tony!" I stopped him and grabbed his hands. "Tell me what's wrong."

He hung his head and let out a horrible sob.

"Zhang has my son again."

I comforted Tony for the next hour, trying to process what he had just told me.

It was well beyond midnight at this point, but I wasn't tired in the slightest. I still had so many questions.

"Tony, are you willing to keep talking about this?" I asked gently. "I want to help James, but I don't want to upset you."

Tony sniffled. "It's fine. What do you want to know?"

"Well, first, I need to know how the police are involved."

"Doc, you have to understand, this organization caters to the elite, wealthy, and powerful — politicians and CEOs. People who have the money and connections to pay off law enforcement."

Hours ago, this would have just sounded like another paranoid conspiracy. But now I believed every word he spoke.

"Zhang keeps collateral on all of them," Tony continued. "The Glade Farm Boys aren't victims — they're perpetrators. You saw number 93, right?"

"Yes, that was Sam."

"Number 93 was *Arthur*," he corrected me. "Every photo captures one of her *clients*. There have been hundreds of them over the years, and she keeps them all locked up in her desk."

"We have to get those pictures!" I said. "With all that evidence, we could finally end this."

"It's not that simple," said Tony. "Zhang keeps that key around her neck every second of the day. Those photos are her lifeline if anything ever goes wrong. And she's been getting more paranoid since I let those kids escape."

"Does Zhang know you were the one releasing them?"

Tony let out a small laugh through his nose. "She had her suspicions. That's why she's been purging everyone."

"Purging?"

"You saw what she did to Arthur, after he claimed he was 'reformed'. And then there was that drug addict kid, Don. He had plenty of drug connections, so she was grooming him to replace Bernard. But he was having none of it — so she killed the kid."

"And Chase..." I pondered out loud. "He was supposed to replace you."

"Yes," said Tony. "It was only a matter of time."

"How did you get involved in the first place?" I asked.

"Extortion," he said. "After I went public about SlapDot, they put me in here to shut me up. And then they—"

He let out a pained sigh.

"It's okay, Tony." I touched his arm sling gently. "Take your time."

Tony cleared his throat. "James was never supposed to get caught in the middle of this. But they... They kidnapped him. And used him as leverage."

"Leverage?"

He hung his head. "They promised not to sell him, as long as I did what they said."

"Jesus, Tony... I'm sorry."

I didn't know what else to say.

If we were going to fight this, we would need help from the

outside.

"Zach."

I gave him a quick hug and sat down.

He glanced at the bandage on my ear. "Elliot, what happened...?"

"It's a long story," I said. "Listen, I have something big for you. There's a pedophile ring—"

"Did you take the OraQuick test?" asked Zach, ignoring me. "Are you taking meds?"

I stared at him. "Did you hear what I just said? Zach, there's a *pedophile ring* operating out of this prison."

He looked at me with a mix of pity and apprehension. "Elliot..."

I gave him an irritable sigh. "When the fuck are you going to start taking me seriously?"

"I do take you seriously!" he protested. "I'm serious about your safety and health."

"I don't give a fuck about my health!" I snapped. "There are kids being abused and murdered!"

He shook his head and pushed his chair back. "I can't do this."

"Do what?" I leaned forward. "You don't believe me?"

"I don't know what to believe anymore!" He threw his arms up in the air. "First, you got HIV from a patient, then you seem to be missing an ear, and now you're telling me there's a pedophile ring in prison? For Christ's sake, Elliot, you're a therapist! Doesn't this pattern concern you?"

"What pattern?" I demanded.

"These outlandish stories!" he said in exasperation. "And it's not like this is the first time. Your entire court case was centered around blaming a nonexistent cult for kidnapping your assistant—"

"I knew it!" I slammed the table. "I knew you never believed me. You haven't been looking for Noah at all, have you?"

He took a deep breath and looked down. "No. I haven't."

I felt my blood boiling. "You're a shit friend and a shit human being."

"Elliot, there's a psychiatrist in this prison," he said anxiously. "You should talk with her."

"SHE'S THE ONE—" I lowered my voice. "She's the one running the fucking pedophile ring!"

Zach shook his head sadly and stood up from his chair.

I wanted to jump across the table and attack him, but there were kids in danger, and that was all I cared about anymore.

"Zach, you don't have to believe me, but look up Tony Singer, okay?" I said. "He's my cellmate, and his son was taken by this pedophile ring."

Zach turned around and frowned. "Tony Singer, from the SlapDot bombing?"

"Yes."

He shook his head. "That's not possible."

"Yes it is!" I said. "Just look into his son."

"No, I mean, it's not possible that he's your cellmate."

"What are you talking about?"

"I covered the SlapDot story," said Zach "Tony Singer was diagnosed with PTSD. He was stuck in denial and invented those conspiracies as a way to cope with his grief. He ended up in a mental hospital on the West Coast."

"Well, he must have been moved to this prison."

"No, he's out now. He does TED Talks about PTSD." Zach turned to leave. "Whoever your cellmate is, he's not Tony Singer."

PART THREE

The next morning, I awoke to the sound of my own choking.

It took me another moment to realize that Tony's hand was locked tight around my neck.

"Tony!" I gasped.

His eyes were closed, like he was asleep, but his grip got tighter until I couldn't breathe anymore.

"Tony!" I choked again, struggling to get away from him. "Tony, stop!"

I threw one last desperate punch at his jaw, and his eyes finally opened.

He looked at me for a second, then his hand, and then released his grip.

"What the fuck, Tony?" I massaged my neck.

"Sorry," he said quickly. "Must have been a nightmare."

"Some nightmare..." I grumbled. "Jesus."

But then I took a second look, and saw that his arm sling was cast aside next to the bed.

"Tony," I said. "Your sling — why'd you take it off?"

He got a horrible look of dread on his face. Then he hurried over to the sling and secured his left arm back inside of it.

"Chem trails..." he muttered under his breath. "Fucking chem trails."

I was about to start telling him that mind-control chem trails weren't real, but then I took another glance at his hand and realized something...

My heart started to race.

Could it be possible?

While Tony was out getting some fresh air, I rummaged through his belongings on the desk.

Nothing but crossword puzzles and angry letters to victims and families of various mass tragedies.

Next, I started tearing apart his bed. Nothing under the pillows, the bed, or inside the sheets.

"Doc? What are you doing?"

I jumped when I saw Tony at the cell door.

"Cleaning," I said.

"No you're not." He scanned the room. "You're looking through my stuff."

I swallowed, and prepared to confront him with my bizarre theory.

"Is — Is your real name Richard Scott?"

"Of course not," he scoffed. "I'm Tony Singer."

"Tony Singer is a famous public speaker," I said. "He's not in prison. But Richard Scott is."

Tony's face started going red. "I already told you, he's in cell block B!"

"Did you strangle your own son?"

"SHUT UP!" he shouted. "SHUT UP!"

He put his hands over his ears like a child.

"I'm not saying you did it on purpose!" I said. "What if it was an accident?"

He slowly lowered his hands and looked at me. "What do you mean?"

"You attacked me this morning," I said.

"It was a nightmare."

"No," I said. "You were sound asleep, but your hand was wide awake. Like it had a mind of its own."

He looked at his left arm in the sling and stared at it nervously.

"What are you getting at?"

"Have you ever heard of Alien Hand Syndrome?"

He shook his head. "No."

"It's a very unusual condition where the patient's hand seems to be acting on its own. Even when you're conscious, you may find it doing things without your permission."

"No," he mumbled again. "I'm Tony Singer."

"What if you're not?" I said. "What if you're Richard Scott, but you took on this Tony Singer identity because you couldn't cope with what happened to your son? What if those mind-controlling chem trails are actually a rare psychological disorder?"

"Fuck off, doc." He stepped closer to me. "Stop playing therapist with me. I'm not your patient."

"Richard, we can work through that trauma. I can help you see that it wasn't your fault."

"I said, FUCK. OFF."

"Richard—"

"STOP CALLING ME RICHARD!" He lunged at me. "I'M TONY SINGER, AND THE SLAPDOT BOMBING WAS STAGED. THEY MADE THE WHOLE THING UP! THEN THEY KIDNAPPED MY SON AND PUT HIM IN A PEDO RING! "

"Your son is gone." I pulled him into a tight hug as he tried to punch me. "Dr. Zhang is using your grief to extort you over a son who is already gone."

"NO!"

"You're saving these boys to make up for your son," I continued. "You're doing something good, but Dr. Zhang is using you. That's what she does. She seeks out patients that she can exploit."

"NO!" he screamed, trying to get away. "GET THE FUCK AWAY FROM ME."

But I held him tighter, and began repeating the same words, over and over:

"It's okay, Richard. It's okay. You didn't mean to. You had no control."

Finally, he stopped struggling and collapsed onto my shoulders with a gut-wrenching cry.

We stayed like that for a long time, until I realized something very concerning.

"Wait a minute…" I pulled away. "If you're Richard Scott — the disposer — then who's the copy cat?"

He frowned. "What?"

"Who's the one brainwashing kids and whispering into my ear in solitary? It wasn't you, so who was it?"

Tony — or Richard — let out a sigh and scratched his head.

"I don't know who he is, but I've heard Bernard talking about him. Apparently he absorbs personalities like a sponge, based on psychological profiles provided by Zhang. Bernard said he's dangerous as hell."

"Dangerous?" I repeated. "How?"

"Because he doesn't just copy them. He believes he *is* them. I'll never forget what Bernard said about him — gave me the fucking spooks."

"What did he say?" I pressed.

Richard went quiet for a second, and then said:

"If you gave this freak a biography on Osama Bin Laden, he'd try to bring down the Freedom Tower."

"HELP! SOMEONE HELP ME!"

I bolted out of bed to see Richard slamming on the cell door. Within seconds, Pickowitz appeared at our cell door.

"What's going on in here?"

"Harper is trying to turn me against Dr. Zhang!" Richard shouted. "He's planning to—"

"What the fuck, Richard?" I shouted.

Pickowitz grabbed the baton from his belt. "On the ground. Both of you."

We did as he said. He entered the cell and restrained us.

"Alright, boys. Come with me. I think Dr. Zhang is still here."

I groaned as we both stood up and followed him to her office.

When we arrived, Dr. Zhang was already standing in the doorway.

"You can take off the handcuffs, Pickowitz..." she spoke softly.

"Are you sure?" said Pickowitz. "Tinfoil said something

about Harper plotting against you."

Dr. Zhang looked over to me with an amused smile.

"*Hmmm*... I can't say that I'm surprised." Then she turned back to Pickowitz. "But I prefer to treat my patients without restraints."

He nodded and removed the handcuffs.

"I'll be right outside if you need anything."

"Thank you, Pickowitz." Dr. Zhang smiled again and motioned for both of us to come in.

We took seats at opposite ends of the couch, and Richard got started immediately.

"Harper is trying to turn me against you! But I swear, I've been doing everything you said. I've been keeping an eye on him. I've been reporting back to the guards. Please—" He begged. "Please, just don't hurt James."

"James *isn't* your son," I hissed back. "She has no leverage over you!"

"Mr. Harper..." Dr. Zhang was twirling the key around her neck. "It's become increasingly clear that you are a danger to the inmates of this prison. Fortunately, Tony here is—"

"His name is Richard," I said, and then repeated: "*Richard.*"

"STOP CALLING ME THAT!" Richard jumped up. "HE KEEPS CALLING ME RICHARD. I DON'T KNOW WHAT THE FUCK IS WRONG WITH HIM!"

"I know, Tony, my dear..." she said, feigning sympathy. "Mr. Harper is a liar and a very bad man."

"Your name is RICHARD." I stood up as well. "And until you face that fact, you're going to be unhappy and confused—"

"FUCK OFF, HARPER!"

He charged at me, and the two of us began brawling.

"That's enough!" Dr. Zhang hurried over to us. "Stop it right now, or you'll both be going to solitary."

I held Richard on the ground and hit him repeatedly in the stomach. Then he rolled me over and started punching me.

"ENOUGH!"

Dr. Zhang tried to pull him off me, but he kicked her in the face — hard. She let out a cry and fell to the ground, and then

Richard jumped on top of her.

"PICKOWITZ!" she shouted.

Pickowitz rushed into the room and yanked Richard away from Dr. Zhang.

"FUCK ALL OF YOU!" Richard screamed. "THE SLAPDOT BOMBING NEVER HAPPENED. IT'S ALL PART OF THEIR PLAN TO CONTROL US!"

"Get him OUT!" said Dr. Zhang, covering her bloodied nose. "I need to get some cotton balls from the infirmary."

Richard turned to me and yelled one last time:

"THE SLAPDOT BOMBING NEVER HAPPENED!"

Then he mouthed "*good luck*" and spat on my legs.

Pickowitz grabbed him and marched him out of the room.

"You." Dr. Zhang glowered at me. "Don't you go anywhere."

She trailed Pickowitz and Richard out of the office, slamming the door behind her.

Heart racing, I reached between my legs where Richard had spat.

And there it was — exactly as planned:

The key from Dr. Zhang's necklace.

End of Patient File: The Snake

Dr. Harper Therapy Company Retreat

The Snake

Finally, we heard sirens wailing in the distance.

"Noah, can you go wave them down?" I asked. "And see if they have a towel to dry him off?"

"Sure," said Noah, waving to James. "Be right back, buddy!"

While we waited for Noah and the police, I knelt down next to James.

"James, are there any other animals you want to tell me about?"

He glanced nervously in Noah's direction.

"He'll be back in a minute," I said reassuringly. "But you can trust me. I just want to make sure all of the animals get punished for hurting you and your friends."

He looked up. "You're going to punish them?"

"Yes," I said. "I promise."

He kicked a bit of sand around, and then mumbled: "The snake."

"What did you say?" I asked. "Snake?"

"Yes." He hung his head. "She says that my mom hates me. She says that my mom will never come look for me because I am a sllll—ut. What does that mean?"

I cringed as he sounded out the word.

"She was lying," I said quickly, but then I frowned. "Wait a minute, the snake is a *girl*? Are you sure?"

"Yes," he said. "She's in charge of them all. She bosses them around, and she yells at them."

"Is she mad?"

"Really mad," he said. "Boys keep running away, and she thinks an animal is helping them."

"James, did an animal help you escape?"

He nodded. "The dragon."

I could see Noah and a police officer approaching.

"The one who burns boys?" I said urgently.

"He woke me up," said James. "He put this shirt on me and told me to run. And he told me not to trust—"

"What have we got here, little guy?" The police officer ducked under the dock with us.

"Not to trust who?" I pressed James.

"Let's get you home," said the policeman, wrapping a towel around James. "Your parents were worried sick."

"He has parents?" I asked.

"Yep. Name is James Allen," said the officer. "His parents filed a missing persons report this afternoon. Lost him in the storm."

"Aren't you excited to go home?" Noah bent down and smiled at James.

"Noah," I said. "I think we should stay with him."

"Not to worry," said the officer. "He'll be safe with me. Come on, James, let's get you home to your family."

"Can you give us their contact information?" I asked. "I'm a therapist, and he's told us some very concerning stories. I'd like to just follow up, if that's okay."

"Of course," said the police officer. "His parents said they would love a chance to thank you in person."

I let out a sigh of relief.

He scrolled through his phone and shared the number with me. I typed it out in my phone as "James - Parents" and set a reminder to call them later.

"Thank you," I said.

I watched as Noah said his goodbyes and briefly concluded the balloon story. For some reason, I really didn't feel comfortable letting James leave our sight, but that was probably just my paranoid side coming out. Plus, later I would be able to share all of my concerns with his parents.

We waved as James walked away with the police officer, and he waved back. It was good to see him smiling again. Before long, the two of them disappeared from sight.

Then it was just Noah and I, standing beneath the dripping dock. It was getting pretty dark, but at least the rain was starting to slow down.

"He was such a sweet kid," said Noah quietly. "I really liked him."

"He liked you too," I said. "You almost became a dad tonight."

Noah laughed. "I would have liked that."

"You're a natural," I said. "Someday, you're going to be an incredible father."

Noah blushed.

As the waves came crashing in around us, he moved a bit closer to me.

"Doc, can I ask you something?"

My heart churned. I knew what was coming, and it wasn't a discussion I was ready to have.

I cleared my throat. "Not today, Noah."

He winced, nodded, and took a small step away from me.

"Come on, let's pack our things," I said. "It's time to go home."

Human Trafficking

Human Trafficking

PART ONE

I fumbled with the key and unlocked Dr. Zhang's desk drawer.

Inside, I found various patient files, along with a folder full of polaroids.

I took a quick glance, but had to look away almost immediately. Inside was the photo of Sam, along with hundreds of other horrifying pictures. I didn't have the time or stomach to look through them all. So instead, I grabbed everything and shoved it inside my pants.

Then I locked the desk drawer, kicked the key under her desk, and hurried back to the couch.

"Mr. Harper…"

I jumped as Dr. Zhang entered the room, holding some ice to her nose.

"Needless to say, you've been a horrible nuisance to my operation here," she said. "You've made it clear that you won't cease with your relentless disruption, and so I've put in a recommendation for your transfer."

"You're transferring me?"

"Yes," she said. "You'll be moved tomorrow morning. Pickowitz will escort you back to your cell to gather your things."

"Okay." I stood up and walked to the door.

"And Mr. Harper?"

"Yes?"

She tilted her head. "If you're thinking of... talking... about what you learned in this prison, I would seriously reconsider. Your life in the next prison can be very good, or very bad, depending on my request."

I nodded. "I don't care anymore. I just want to get the hell out of here."

She gave me one last smile. "That's very good to hear, Mr. Harper."

I knocked on the door and Pickowitz walked me back to my cell.

As he locked the cell door behind him, I ran over to the desk, reached into my pants, and began organizing everything into folders. Then I hurried back to the door and whispered: "Pickowitz!"

He turned back and said, "Yeah?"

I took a deep breath.

"My friend, Zach. Is he paying you to help me out?"

Pickowitz gave me a wink. "I don't know what you're talking about."

"Okay, good."

I shoved a manilla folder through the bars.

"What's this?" he asked, taking it.

"An important secret," I said. "If you don't believe me, look inside yourself. But don't show anyone else. Not until I'm back."

He raised his eyebrows. "Back from where?"

I looked him in the eye. "Trust me."

He nodded and put the folder in his shirt.

As he walked away, I let out a sigh of relief and went back to the desk.

Now, all I needed was a bit of good luck.

"Where are the photos, Mr. Harper?"

Dr. Zhang stood at my cell door with a smile, but she did not seem her usual calm self.

I walked slowly to the door to face her.

"I gave them to someone who will send them to the FBI if I don't check in every hour, on the hour."

It was a bit of an exaggeration, but she didn't need to know that.

She tilted her head stiffly. "Mr. Harper, I can't help but wonder—"

"No," I interrupted her. "I'm calling the shots now. You're not in control anymore."

She pursed her lips. "What do you want?"

"I hear you take your favorite inmates on field trips," I said. "Let's go for one now."

Her eyes met mine. I could practically see the gears spinning in her brain as she tried to manipulate the situation. "I can't make that happen right now, but if you'd like to wait—"

"Your fingerprints were all over those photos, weren't they?" I said. "What's the charge for possession of child pornography? How about child sex slavery?"

She glared at me.

"We're leaving now," I said. "Call a guard and escort me from my cell."

Her smile faded completely. She waited a few seconds, and then she did as I said.

Within minutes, we were walking down the halls to the building's exit.

"Elliot Harper," she said to the guards at the front gates. "He's joining me for a mental health retreat."

"Of course, Dr. Zhang."

It was incredible how everyone at this prison just did what she said. But it wasn't surprising, given the political figures and lawmakers in her collection of photos.

As we stepped past the walls into the cool night air, I looked up at the stars and my heart lit up. I hadn't seen the stars since I got here.

"This way."

I followed Dr. Zhang to her car and stepped into the passenger side.

Neither of us spoke during the extremely awkward car ride. We drove about ten minutes, before she pulled off to a side road and parked in an empty lot next to an eighteen wheeler.

"Where are we?" I said. "I want to see where you keep the kids."

She glared at me. "This *is* where I keep them."

My eyes went wide as I saw the text on the side of the truck: *Glade Farm Milk*

"You keep them in a truck?"

I was expecting some sort of abandoned warehouse, or an underground bunker.

"For transport," she said, getting out of the car. "We deliver them to the clients."

"Jesus," I muttered. "Like some fucked up version of Prime."

She checked her phone briefly and I could have sworn I saw her smile, but then she led me to the truck and unlocked the freight container.

I hopped in after her.

Inside, both sides were lined with two levels of small covered cages, at least fifty in total. It looked like some sort of animal shelter.

My heart sank. "Are they... Are they in there?"

"Yes," said Dr. Zhang, glancing at her watch. "They're currently sedated. Now, what do you want?"

"I want you to drive the truck to my friend's house," I said. She scoffed. "What?"

"Here's the address," I said, shoving a piece of paper at her. "Let's go, now."

"Mr. Harper..."

"It's *Doctor* Harper."

She gave me a forced smile. "Dr. Harper... What exactly is your friend going to do? Why not just call the police?"

I laughed. "Nice try. I know about your police connections. We're going to his house. Now."

She gave me a curt nod.

But as we returned to the back of the truck, I heard another car pull up.

"Who is that?" I demanded.

"I don't know," she said.

"Bullshit," I said. "Who the hell is that? Did you call someone?"

But my question was quickly answered when Pickowitz emerged in the cargo container with us, carrying the manilla folder.

Dr. Zhang was beaming.

"Mr. Harper... I believe you've met Todd Pickowitz. In fact, the two of you were neighbors in solitary. As I'm sure you learned, he has a very unique skillset when it comes to mirroring identities."

I groaned.

"That's right," she said triumphantly. "You gave the photos to my most loyal colleague. Please come along and give me the folder."

Pickowitz nodded and walked over, handing the folder to her.

She greedily tore it open, and then frowned.

"What is this?" she said, flipping through torn-out pages of a notebook. "Pickowitz, these aren't the photos. They're journal entries from that Zombie kid — Chase Collins."

"Yo, that's what Doctor H told me to read..." said Pickowitz in Chase's voice.

Dr. Zhang looked at him in confusion. "What are you doing? Why are you talking like that?"

I stepped forward. "I know who Pickowitz is."

She turned to me and frowned. "How?"

"A long time ago, I met one of your victims," I said. "A little boy named James. And he described a 'minty man' who stole personalities."

She scoffed. "So what?"

Pickowitz smelled his armpits. "Yo, I do smell minty!"

"He reeks of menthol," I said. "I could smell it from my

141

cell."

"So you turned him into an idiotic college jock," Dr. Zhang laughed at me. "Good for you. Pickowitz — or Chase — whoever the fuck you are. Search Mr. Harper for the photos."

I took a deep breath.

"Dr. Zhang, you should be more careful about the tricks you teach to monsters."

She gave me a puzzled look, and then her eyes went wide.

But she was too late.

I pointed my finger at Dr. Zhang, and shouted to Pickowitz: "BULK UP, SKINNY FAGGOT."

"No!" Dr. Zhang shrieked.

Pickowitz lunged forward and bit her in the neck.

She let out a scream and fell to the ground as Pickowitz began attacking her torso.

I knelt down to her level and watched as blood spurted from her neck.

"*Help...*" she choked. "*You're not a murderer.*"

I held her hand in mine, because nobody should pass onto the next life alone.

I saw the panic in her eyes — the panic of a person who knew they were going to die.

"*You're a protector! You see the good in others. You believe in redemption.*"

For the next several minutes, Pickowitz continued to tear her apart and I listened as she desperately spewed various methods of manipulation to garner my sympathy.

I did not respond.

Instead, I simply waited and watched as she bled out.

As Pickowitz fed on Dr. Zhang's corpse, I hit him in the skull with a rock by one of the cages. He fell to the ground, writhing and groaning. I leaned forward and fastened his hands behind his back with some rope. Then I tied his legs together as well.

"Sorry," I muttered. "When you get back to prison, read up

on mindfulness. Learn to become comfortable with that empty feeling, rather than trying to fill the void. Eventually, it will reveal its truth to you, and you will be free of this miserable addiction."

He continued moaning as I rolled him toward the back of the truck. I hopped off and carried him over to the side of the road.

I had just used a person's mental illness against them, which put me on the same level as Zhang, but there was no turning back now. So I jumped back up to the bed of the truck and pushed Zhang over the edge.

Her mutilated body hit the pavement with a sickening crack.

And finally, I held my breath and prepared myself for the worst part.

I turned to the dozens of cages around me and began ripping the curtains open.

What I saw will haunt my dreams for the rest of my life.

Young boys, some naked, some barely clothed — caged like dogs, surrounded by filth and feces. Not even enough space to stand up. All of them seemed to be sedated.

I kept tearing away the curtains as my heart screamed in agony.

And finally, I found James.

Dirty, malnourished, and alone.

So alone.

We had every chance to save him from this living hell, and instead we returned him to his abusers.

Tears welled in my eyes, and I suddenly felt the overwhelming urge to throw up.

I bolted out the back of the truck and went into the woods.

I needed to run — to sprint. Anything to release the unbearable anxiety gnawing at my core.

And so I ran.

I ran through the woods, and I screamed.

I screamed every curse word I could think of. The sounds came deep from within my soul. Anguish, heartbreak, and rage.

So much rage.

What kind of God could let children go through this kind of

torture and humiliation?

"FUCK YOU!" I screamed into the sky, tears streaming down my face. "FUCK YOU!"

I tripped over a root and fell down at the base of a tree.

I tried to scream again, but instead I vomited all over the ground.

As I laid there panting — alone in the woods — I looked up at the night sky one last time.

The constellations sparkled, but I could not see beautiful things anymore.

PART TWO

Forgotten Children, Forgotten Man

*Zach Johnson is an award-winning investigative journalist with The Sun.
After breaking the Glade Farm story last month, hundreds of high-profile
individuals have been arrested. Johnson will detail the entire investigation
in a major book deal coming this fall.*

You know the Glade Farm victims.

You've seen their faces. You've learned of their unimaginable
trauma. You've seen them reunited with their families. You've
heard many of their harrowing stories.

You know their abusers.

You've seen billionaires, congressmen, and celebrities
handcuffed on live television. You've seen their attempts to
circumvent justice with money. You've seen those attempts fail.

You know the paper that broke the story.

You've seen the front-page Sunday exposé that shook a
country. You've seen us publish the names of every single
perpetrator, despite repeated attempts to silence us.

But you still don't know the man who unraveled it all.

One month ago, a prisoner by the name of Dr. Elliot Harper
approached me with concerns about a child sex-trafficking ring.
He told me that prison inmates and staff were using criminal
connections to abuse hundreds of boys. He told me that he had
been given a life-threatening illness for trying to expose the
conspiracy.

I dismissed his story.

His outlandish claims of a pedophile ring reminded me of his outlandish claims of his own innocence.

One year ago, Elliot was given a life sentence for kidnapping, torture, and attempted murder. He vehemently denied those accusations, insisting that he was framed by a cult.

Like the rest of the world, I dismissed his story.

But when dozens of boys appeared on my doorstep in the middle of the night, I realized I had made not one — but *two* — horrible mistakes.

If every single one of Elliot's bizarre claims of sex trafficking turned out to be true, what did that mean about his bizarre claims of innocence?

And so, over the past month, I set out to investigate those claims.

What I have found will shock you, just as the Glade Farm story shocked you.

Imagine a deep-web cult that kidnaps and brainwashes homeless people, forcing them to play the role of father, mother, and child for false families.

I have found evidence of this cult, including a homeless father and his daughter who were rescued from their false families.

They were rescued by Dr. Elliot Harper.

In the coming weeks, I will share the findings of my investigation.

I cannot change the court's ruling on Elliot, but I can try to change the court of public opinion. Perhaps once you've seen the evidence yourself, you'll start to reconsider your assumptions — just as I did mine.

It is my hope that someday Elliot will feel safe turning himself in, so that he may receive a fair trial. I am confident that he will be exonerated.

But until that point, I understand why he must hide.

I have known Elliot since we were young boys. He's always been a bossy know-it-all — unyieldingly stubborn, and relentlessly rude too. Let's not forget, this is a man who delivered a truckload of traumatized children at my doorstep with a sticky note that read: "I told you so, fuckface."

But he is a good man. A chaotic good — for sure — but good nonetheless.

Elliot, I hope you will accept my most sincere apology.

I know you enjoy horoscopes, so I will leave you with this week's forecast:

With mercury retrograde in full force, things are quite difficult now. But with the waning moon disappearing on Monday evening, the stars will soon shine bright. Recover from the retrograde with a delightful viewing of constellations like Ursa Major and Horologium.

The weight will soon pass, and your dreams will come true.

———————————————————//————————————————

I put the newspaper back on the stand. I liked coming to this drugstore at 6am to buy food and supplies for my tent. It was always empty and the owner was blind, making it one of the few places that I felt comfortable being in public (wearing a hat, of course).

"Mercury retrograde...?" I muttered to myself, still staring at the front page.

What the hell was Zach talking about? He knew that I hated horoscopes.

Not to mention, the two constellations couldn't be more different. Ursa Major was the brightest and best-known constellation in the sky. Meanwhile, Horologium was an obscure collection of stars in in the Southern Celestial Hemisphere — not even remotely visible here.

When I first met Zach in church choir, he only knew the Big Dipper, which he thought was the same as Ursa Major. And I remember teaching him about Horologium, even though we couldn't see it. I wouldn't have bothered mentioning it, but the constellation represents a clock, and we were at the top of—

I froze.

Zach and I used to spend our evenings watching the stars together — from the church's clock tower.

Was this some sort of hidden message to me?

"Monday evening... Clock... Big Dipper..." I thought out loud. Holy shit. He wanted to meet at our old spot tomorrow night.

I quickly gathered my things and hurried up to the cash register. Nearby, I spotted a display of OraQuick HIV tests and felt my heart tighten. If there was ever a sign from above...

After a few moments of hesitation, I bit my lip and grabbed one of the boxes.

But as I paid for my things, I started to get the uncanny feeling that I was being watched. I slowly turned my head to the front door and saw that I was not alone.

A woman and her son were standing there, watching me. As soon as the woman saw me, she looked away and took out her phone.

Fuck.

"Listen, keep the change," I said, shoving $60 at the cashier.

He counted the bills as I grabbed my things and put my head down, trying to look calm and casual as I approached the front door.

I almost made it out the shop, when I heard a nervous: *"Wait!"*

I took a deep breath and stopped in my tracks. I turned around, but did not raise my head. "Yes?"

The woman look terrified.

Would I have to push her in front of her son? Hit her? Run from her? Steal her phone?

Hands shaking, she reached into her purse and took out a huge wad of cash.

And then, to my shock, she handed it to me and whispered: *"Thank you."*

Back at my tent, I opened the OraQuick box and read the instructions:

Gently swab your upper and lower gums. Then insert swab into test tube and wait 20 minutes for results. A pink line indicates a positive test.

I quickly swiped the test swab along my upper and lower gums, and then put it inside the test tube.

I took a deep breath and closed my eyes. I'm not really the praying type, since I don't think any deity has the power to change whether or not I was already infected with HIV. It either happened or it didn't.

So instead, for the next twenty minutes, I did something I hadn't done in nearly a year.

I meditated.

I simply watched all of my anxious thoughts, spinning around in circles and trying to fix everything — trying to analyze every possible outcome of this test. The more I observed this frenzied internal dialogue, the less I identified with it.

In the quiet of my mind, I suddenly felt an overwhelming sensation surge through my body. It was a feeling I hadn't known since childhood — lightness and freedom — connected with every single thing around me. There was no separation. No punisher in the sky. No victim below.

As the heaviness inside of me dissolved, it was almost as if I could feel the breeze of the forest blowing straight through my body.

"*Stay*," I quietly begged this feeling. "*Please, stay.*"

And then I heard something.

Maybe it was a spiritual experience, or maybe I was talking to myself... Or maybe I'd finally lost my mind. But I swear I heard the following word, clear as day:

Surrender.

My eyes shot open and I looked around frantically.

"What does that mean?" I asked out loud. "Like surrender to the police?"

But the feeling was already gone. Once again, my body was heavy, and my mind was racing. For the next several minutes, I tried to recreate that fleeting feeling, but nothing seemed to work.

And before I knew it, twenty minutes had passed.

So I held my breath, opened the tube, and read the results.

PART THREE

The next night, I showed up at the bellower and saw Zach looking out over the ledge.

I walked up behind him and mumbled, "So I'm a bossy know-it-all?"

He turned around with a big smiled and clapped me on the shoulder.

"Elliot — you came!"

"Of course."

I couldn't believe I was standing here with him again, after all these years.

"Listen," said Zach, as we turned to face the stars. "I've got a few things I need to tell you."

"Alright..." I said. "Are you going to keep me in suspense?"

"What do you want first?" he asked. "The good news, medium news, or bad news?"

I laughed. "I could definitely use some good news right now."

"Okay then!"

I could tell he was really excited about something. He walked over to the second stairway and started waving his hands. What the hell was down there?

A few seconds later, my heart raced as a I saw a figure step out from the stairwell.

But when the figure's face was illuminated by the starlight, my heart felt something else entirely.

"Noah?"

He sprinted over to me and pulled me into a huge hug. "Doc!"

I hugged him back, and we stayed like that for what felt like an eternity. It was the first non-threatening human contact I'd known in a very long time.

When our hug finally ended, I looked into his eyes and shook my head in disbelief. He looked exactly the same as the last time I saw him.

All I could manage to say was: "*How?*"

"You two have a lot of catching up to do," said Zach, touching our backs. "I'm going to give you some time."

He stepped into the stairway, leaving me alone with Noah.

"Noah, how are you here right now?" I asked. "What happened to you?"

"Your friend, Zach!" said Noah cheerfully. "He found where Kierra was keeping me. I'm not sure how. I think he might be a genius."

I laughed. "Yeah, he definitely is."

"What about you? How was prison?"

"It was fine," I lied. "I'm just so relieved that you're okay. That was all that mattered to me."

Noah blushed.

"And I'm really sorry about how I left things between us," I continued. "I was trying to protect you, but I fucked everything up."

"Wait…" He tilted his head. "So you *didn't* want me to leave on your birthday?"

"No," I said gently. "No, of course not. That was… It was the best night of my life."

"Oh!" His eyes lit up. "Okay! Uh — then would you like to go on a date?"

"A date?" I sputtered. "You — want to go on a date — with me?"

"Yeah!" he said. Then he thought for a moment and added, "But if it becomes a relationship, it has to be mutual. I've been working a lot on my boundaries and self-respect, so no more bossing me around."

I felt a sudden anxiety taking over. I actually would have loved to go on a date, but he didn't know my secret yet...

"Noah—"

"I want decisions to be equal, because relationships are supposed to be equal. And no offense, but sometimes you make really bad decisions."

"Noah!"

He blushed again, and in a moment, all his confidence vanished.

"I'm sorry," he said quietly, looking down in embarrassment. "You don't want to. That's okay."

"No, it's not that," I said quickly. "It's just... I—"

"What is it, doc?"

I took a deep breath and finally mumbled the words I had been dreading:

"I have HIV."

His eyes widened.

I opened my mouth, preparing to answer how I got it. I needed him to know it didn't come from some sort of prison relationship. I couldn't even imagine what he must have thought of me. God, this wasn't fair. I had dreamed of this moment, and now Noah was looking at me like... that.

But before I could string together a sentence, Noah spoke up again.

"Well, we need to get you started on treatment! Especially early on, I've heard it's really important to get on medications so you can live a healthy life. You know, there's a clinic back at home that helped my friend Ryan through this. I bet they would be willing to help you discreetly too. And if not, I can just tell them I need the medications for myself..."

As I listened to him ramble on about HIV, I frowned. Was his only concern for my health?

"So..." Noah finished. "What about the other stuff? Do you want to go on a date?"

"Wait—" I raised my eyebrows. "You still *want* to?"

"Of course," he said earnestly. "Why wouldn't I?"

"You don't... You're not concerned about how I got HIV?

Or why I don't have an ear? Or—"

"Well, it doesn't matter to me," he said gently. "I'm just so happy to see you again."

It took a few moments for me to realize that I had no need for all of the walls, analyses, and explanations I had planned.

So instead, I let it all go and surrendered to the kindness that had always been there in front of me.

"Oh — okay," I stammered. "I'd love to go on a date."

His smile could have rivaled the world's happiest golden retriever.

Noah and I caught up for another fifteen minutes, before Zach stepped out of the stairwell and approached us

"Alright, Elliot," he said. "We're a bit short on time tonight. Are you ready for the medium news?"

"Oh, right..." I said unenthusiastically. "There's more."

Zach nodded. "So after you told me about your cellmate, I did some digging on the SlapDot bombing—"

"Oh, you were right about all that," I said. "Singer wasn't my cellmate."

"I know," he said. "But something else came up. SlapDot is planning to host a weeklong festival for social media influencers on a private tropical island."

"Wait a minute..." I said. "Didn't that already fail catastrophically?"

"That was Fyre Festival," said Zach. "This event has virtually unlimited corporate funding, and they've been planning it for a year. It's supposed to be the experience of a lifetime. Every online celebrity is fighting for a ticket."

I rolled my eyes. "Sounds absolutely miserable."

Zach glanced to the left. "Well actually, I was hoping you might join me there."

"What?" I said. "Why the hell would we go to that?"

"I've been digging through some blogs and comments, and I think something bad is going to happen there."

"Like what?" I scoffed. "Someone's going to lose Instagram followers?"

"No, Elliot." He shook his head seriously. "Like *really* bad."

I frowned. "What, like another bombing?"

"I don't know," he said. "But something like that."

"Well, have you gone to the police?"

"Yes," said Zach. "They said it's just a bunch of online trolls, but this doesn't seem like trolling to me. If we don't do something, I think a lot of people are going to die."

"How am I supposed to help with this?"

"Do what you do best," said Zach. "Talk to them. Find out what they know. Learn about their past."

"Zach—"

"Look, Elliot, I'm good at digging stuff up, but you're the one who figures people out. Look at all the stuff that happened in prison. I didn't listen to you, and you were right the whole time. I can't afford to make the same mistakes with this. Please. I need your help."

I took a deep breath. "So you want me to play therapist for a bunch of vapid, mindless narcissists."

Zach nodded.

"Ugh," I said. "Fine. But after this, we're even."

"Fantastic!" he said. "I've already made arrangements for the four of us."

"Four?"

"Ah." Zach gave me a forced smile. "Yes… Now we've reached the bad news."

"Great…" I grumbled.

"I tried to convince him it was a bad idea," said Zach, glancing at Noah. "But… he insisted."

"It's not bad!" said Noah, hurrying over to the stairs. "You can come up now!"

I was surprised to see another shadow step out from the stairwell, but this time it was not a welcomed surprise.

"No." I shook my head. "No, absolutely not."

My insides writhed with hatred as Kierra walked over to me.

"Hi, Dr. Harper."

I ignored her and turned to Noah. "*Noah, what the hell?*"

"Okay, before you get upset, you need to know that she's changed."

"Changed?" I said incredulously. "How?"

"Well, in our time together—"

"She *kidnapped* you!"

"True," he said quickly. "But during that time, she realized I didn't want to resume our relationship. So instead, I helped her learn how to be a good person!"

"Noah..." I groaned. "You can't fix a sociopath with kindness."

"He's telling the truth," said Kierra quietly. "I was resistant at first, but he refused to give up on me."

"Bullshit."

"Doc!" said Noah. "I used a lot of the skills you taught me. And in the process, I gained a lot of self-respect too."

"You're not a therapist!"

"Technically, neither are you anymore," said Zach. Then he saw my glare and muttered: "Sorry."

"Doc, please just trust me?" said Noah. "Remember, we talked about being mutual and equal?"

"Noah, she's dangerous!" I said. "I just don't want you getting hurt."

"She's different now," he said. "I promise. Give her a chance. She promised to be nice to you, and not to make fun of your burnt... thing anymore."

His cheeks went red. He was referring to how Kierra used to mock my history of self-harm.

Kierra stepped forward and extended her hand. "Truce?"

I didn't accept the handshake. "Whatever."

As I looked around the bellower, I shook my head and tried to adjust to my new reality. I was about to be stuck on an island with a self-proclaimed reformed sociopath, my codependent assistant who I was also apparently dating, and the childhood crush who rejected me.

This was my life now.

"So... Is that a yes?" asked Zach.

I sighed. "I'll go with you guys to your stupid island."

All three of them smiled excitedly.

"Alright, let's get out of here," said Zach, handing me a phone. "This is a disposable phone. Use it to communicate before and during the festival. I'll be in touch with travel plans."

I took the phone and followed them down the stairwell.

Zach and Noah went first, with Kierra and I trailing a few paces behind. And then, about halfway down the stairs, Kierra slowed down and turned to me, blocking the steps.

She sniffled and quivered her lips. "I — I just want to say something."

"What?" I snapped.

Then she broke into a smile, gave me a wink, and whispered: "Welcome back, dick burner."

End of Patient File: The Little Wizard

SlapFest Sold Out in Less Than 1 Hour

Earlier today, influencers and online celebrities scrambled to secure their tickets for the first ever SlapDot Festival. Within minutes, the site crashed from the spike in traffic. And within an hour, every ticket was sold.

The lowest tier of tickets started at $5,000. Meanwhile, top models and YouTube personalities boasted of private beachfront villas at $100,000.

Hosted on a private tropical island, the social media giant SlapDot has poured millions into making the event a success. Slated as a tribute to the lives lost in the SlapDot bombing, SlapFest is a "celebration of music, entertainment, and love".

Attendees range from beauty gurus to motivational speakers to body-positive advocates to prankster couples. Throughout the day, hundreds of these influencers took to social media to share photos and videos of their tickets to excite their fans.

In a climate that boasts endless days of sunshine and dramatic thunderstorms at night, guests can choose to enjoy a relaxing beach vacation — or participate in a variety of exciting adventures and events.

The island is home to natural waterfalls, private swimming

holes, and mineral-rich hot springs. SlapDot has already arranged for bungee jumping, snorkeling tours, skydiving, and Jet Ski excursions. Professional chefs will prepare menus and meals for the entire island at a variety of themed restaurants.

The week will end with an exclusive sunset yacht cruise for the highest-profile guests.

To quote the SlapDot CEO: "The setting is absolutely perfect for any content creator looking to generate stunning content and attract new followers. Trust me, you don't want to miss this opportunity."

What would you do for a ticket? Tell us in the comments!

COMMENTS (1,038)

@indygirl397860
Jealous! I would pay my life savings! Too bad that's $200 LOL

@__reagan_USA
Bunch of millennial losers. Get a REAL JOB.

@44bigwatch
Don't most of these "influencers" hate each other? What happens when you stick them on an island together…?

@anonymous9336
There will be a massacre.
And the massacre will be livestreamed.

Thank you for reading the Prison Files.
The Influencer Files are next. If you'd like to read them, please
check out my private practice at:

www.DrHarperTherapy.com

@DrHarperTherapy

Subscribe for new stories and incredible fan art on Reddit:

/r/Dr_Harper

If you enjoyed the book, please consider leaving a review
on Amazon to help others discover my files.